School
Prodigies
Have It
Easy
Even in
Another
World!

3

©Sacraneco

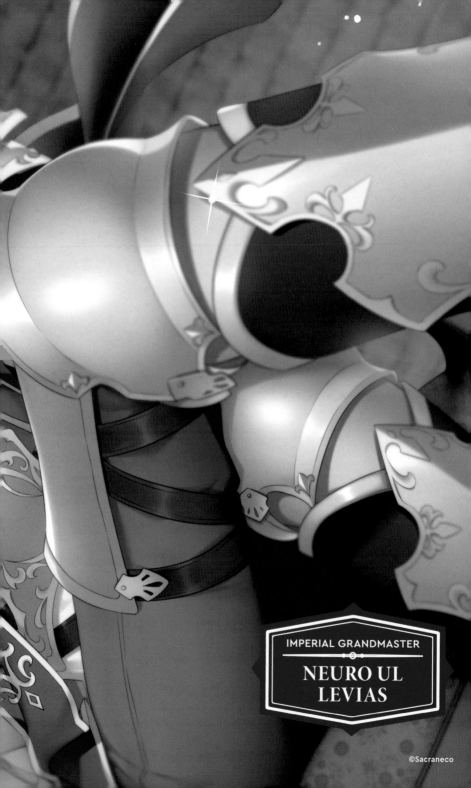

IMPERIAL GRANDMASTER

NEURO UL
LEVIAS

©Sacraneco

CONTENTS

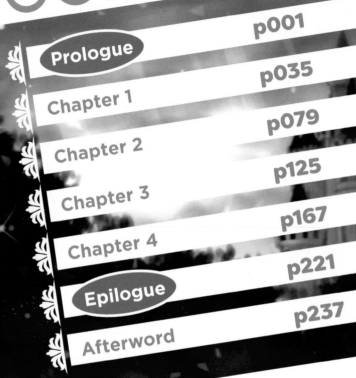

RIKU MISORA
ILLUSTRATION BY
SACRANECO

**High School Prodigies
Have It Easy Even in
Another World!**

©Sacraneco

High School Prodigies Have It Easy Even in Another World!

3

Riku Misora

Illustration by SACRANECO

YEN ON

NEW YORK

©Sacraneco

High School Prodigies Have It Easy Even in Another World! 3

Riku Misora

TRANSLATION BY NATHANIEL HIROSHI THRASHER
COVER ART BY SACRANECO

This book is a work of fiction. Names, characters, places, and incidents are the product of the author's imagination or are used fictitiously. Any resemblance to actual events, locales, or persons, living or dead, is coincidental.

CHOUJIN KOUKOUSEITACHI HA ISEKAI DEMO YOYU DE IKINUKU YOUDESU! vol. 3
Copyright © 2016 Riku Misora
Illustrations copyright © 2016 Sacraneco
All rights reserved.
Original Japanese edition published in 2016 by SB Creative Corp.
This English edition is published by arrangement with SB Creative Corp.,
Tokyo in care of Tuttle-Mori Agency, Inc., Tokyo.

English translation © 2021 by Yen Press, LLC

Yen Press, LLC supports the right to free expression and the value of copyright. The purpose of copyright is to encourage writers and artists to produce the creative works that enrich our culture.

The scanning, uploading, and distribution of this book without permission is a theft of the author's intellectual property. If you would like permission to use material from the book (other than for review purposes), please contact the publisher. Thank you for your support of the author's rights.

Yen On
150 West 30th Street, 19th Floor
New York, NY 10001

Visit us at yenpress.com
facebook.com/yenpress ★ twitter.com/yenpress
yenpress.tumblr.com ★ instagram.com/yenpress

First Yen On Edition: January 2021

Yen On is an imprint of Yen Press, LLC.
The Yen On name and logo are trademarks of Yen Press, LLC.

The publisher is not responsible for websites (or their content) that are not owned by the publisher.

Library of Congress Cataloging-in-Publication Data
Names: Misora, Riku, author. | Sacraneco, illustrator. | Thrasher, Nathaniel Hiroshi, translator.
Title: High school prodigies have it easy even in another world! / Riku Misora ;
illustration by Sacraneco ; translation by Nathaniel Hiroshi Thrasher.
Other titles: Chōjin-Kokoseitachi wa Isekai demo Yoyu de Ikinuku Yōdesu! English
Identifiers: LCCN 2020016894 | ISBN 9781975309725 (v. 1 ; trade paperback) |
ISBN 9781975309749 (v. 2 ; trade paperback) | ISBN 9781975309763 (v. 3 ; trade paperback)
Subjects: CYAC: Fantasy. | Gifted persons—Fiction. | Imaginary places—Fiction | Magic—Fiction.
Classification: LCC PZ7.M6843377 Hi 2020 | DDC [Fic]—dc23
LC record available at https://lccn.loc.gov/2020016894

ISBNs: 978-1-9753-0976-3 (paperback)
978-1-9753-0977-0 (ebook)

1 3 5 7 9 10 8 6 4 2

LSC-C

Printed in the United States of America

❈ Two Wars ❈

Le Luk.

That was the name of the mountain range that cut between the Findolph and Buchwald domains and boasted an elevation of sixteen thousand feet above sea level.

Between its precipitous high-altitude terrain, the wind and water spirit leylines crisscrossing the area, and the constant blizzards that buffeted the region throughout the winter, it was one of the most perilous places in all the northern lands.

In fact, up until about a hundred years ago, when the then-current emperor ordered that a road be built through it as part of his plan to develop the north, Le Luk was so secluded that the people of Buchwald used it to store and preserve their food.

Even now, with the mountain pass established, hardly anybody dared traverse the range during winter.

As a blizzard swept over the frigid mountains, a black serpent slithered along its route.

This winding asp was not one creature but rather was made up of many marching people. It was a long line of men and horses. Clad in furs, *hyuma* and *byuma* alike huddled together as they made their way up the mountain road.

They were the joint punitive force that two of the four northern domains, Buchwald and Archride, had formed to put down the rebellious Order of the Seven Luminaries that had taken over Findolph.

All told, the coalition's forces numbered three thousand strong.

However, the group traveling up the peak was only a third of that total sum.

It took infantry a day and a half to traverse Le Luk in the winter.

In other words, they needed somewhere to stay the night in order to make the trip.

That was where the Le Luk checkpoint came in, but even packed to the gills, it could only house a thousand men at a time.

If they tried sending all three thousand soldiers through Le Luk at once, two thousand of them would've ended up having to make camp outside. Sleeping outside during the colder Le Luk months was a death sentence.

Their commander, Marquis Archride, had chosen to split the army into three groups just small enough for the checkpoint to support, then led the first one toward the rebel-occupied Findolph domain.

However, having a road to support their march did little to change the windy, snowy mountain's brutal terrain.

""""AHHHHHHHHH!!!!""""

Sudden screams erupted from a section of their procession.

An avalanche had started.

Untimely gusts of wind had brought a cascade of snow thundering down from atop a cliff.

Some soldiers hadn't reacted quickly enough, their frightful cries echoing as their last words before being fatally crushed. Others twisted their ankles as those who fled shoved them over in their haste to escape the avalanche. Some of the shrieks came from that group. Different pained exclamations came from those who suffered cracked or broken bones when the soldiers with twisted ankles crashed into them.

While there were a few unfortunates who perished under the wave of heavy snow, far more had been wounded by the domino effect it had caused.

That was hardly surprising, however. The cavalcade was moving so slowly that even avoidable avalanches had become lethal threats.

Merely trying to pass through Le Luk during the winter was a suicide mission. Everyone knew that, yet these poor folks were still being made to march.

The fault for that lay exclusively in the hands of the idiot who refused to wait for the snow to thaw and instead obstinately forced the army to move out while it was still winter—the Fastidious Duke, Oslo el Gustav.

After the fifth avalanche, the soldiers finally started to let slip their frustrations.

"Fuckin' Gustav, sitting pretty in the capital, not knowing a thing about winter in the mountains..."

"Why do we gotta put up with this shit?"

"It's cold...and scary... I can't take this anymore..."

Eventually, the murmurs reached Marquis Archride, who rode at the rear of the vanguard.

"...Shall I shut them up?" offered Kreitzo, the fox-eared and fox-tailed Gold Knight riding beside him.

Archride shook his head.

"Let them yammer. I feel the same way they do."

Archride turned and looked at the faces of the soldiers huddled behind him. All of them were freezing, and they were clearly exhausted after having been forced to march through the ice and snow. Even the sheer absurdity of traveling through Le Luk during the most dangerous time of year seemed to have sapped many warriors of their vigor. Most of all, however, everyone looked fearful that they would be the next ones to fall prey to a large icicle or avalanche.

The fighting hadn't even begun yet, and their morale was already at rock bottom. Archride sensed the same things in himself but was cautious not to let it show. He was cursing Oslo el Gustav just as hard as his charges were.

None doubted Gustav's strength. No other man in the empire held the ranks of both Platinum Knight, the highest knighthood title, and Prime Mage, the highest imperial magecraft title. Archride was also familiar with the tale of how Gustav's Heavenly Fire had burned down an entire Yamato stronghold in a single night. It was only proper that such a man be venerated.

Individual strength and leadership ability were two wholly separate skills, though. Gustav had ordered the army to cross Le Luk no matter the cost and had set a domestic policy that prioritized gold statues and picturesque views so highly it drove his people to starvation. It would've been disingenuous to describe Gustav's statesmanship as anything but utterly incompetent.

Knowing that, Archride had exaggerated his reports to avoid giving Gustav any cause to micromanage the subjugating army, telling him that through wartime conscription, he and Buchwald would raise an army a hundred thousand strong. Unfortunately, the situation had taken the worst turn imaginable. Archride had underestimated exactly how impatient the Fastidious Duke was.

His Grace chose a poor man to grant authority to.

Beneath his thick white beard, Archride bit his lip. The time to complain would end before long, however.

Once they made it through the mountains, they'd be in rebel-controlled territory—the battlefield.

"…"

Archride's thoughts turned toward the enemy awaiting them.

Honestly, I don't know what to make of them…but I know they're not to be taken lightly.

A distant relative of Archride's in the Findolph domain had informed him that Marquis Findolph had been captured and that the Dormundt metropolis had fallen completely under the control of a religious group called the Seven Luminaries, which preached a message of universal equality.

The empire didn't devote many resources to protecting it, but Findolph was still an imperial domain. Seizing it had been a substantial military feat. It was nothing to casually dismiss. What's more, there was word that the individual claiming to be the Seven Luminaries' God had performed feats the likes of which not even magic had yet achieved. People spoke of things like a mountain vanishing, only to reappear a moment later. The deity's angel attendants were also rumored to possess the power to create metal that was lighter than wood and to cure any wound or ailment known to man.

It was with such impossible powers that the Seven Luminaries had won over the public's hearts and minds. Archride had received notice that the enemy had even gotten some nobles to join their cause and that peace and order in Findolph were far greater than they'd been under the previous lord's rule.

This isn't just a ragtag band fed up with the system…

Archride had no intention of believing in deities. He could not deny, however, that the opposition employed strange abilities, utilized the power of religion to unify the masses, and had such a strong political vision that even those of the former ruling class were acquiescing. They were well on their way to shaping themselves into an actual nation.

Furthermore, according to the guide who'd helped Silver Knight Inzaghi, the captain of Findolph's knight order, flee through Le Luk, one of the Seven Luminaries wielded a katana—the signature weapon of the Yamato Empire.

Archride had no idea what to make of any of it.

Damn it all… If we could've just waited for spring…

The "hundred thousand" number Archride had reported to Gustav may have been an exaggeration, but if they'd gone by his original plan and waited for the thaw, he and Buchwald could've certainly had fifty thousand soldiers mobilized and ready to stream ceaselessly into the Findolph domain.

Not knowing the scope of the opposing forces meant it was crucial to hit them with the greatest force they could muster. Thanks to Gustav, however, they had to bring their troops through midwinter Le Luk, where they could only deploy a thousand men a day.

Archride's plan to overwhelm the enemy with numbers was in shambles. Now they had no choice but to act with the utmost caution. Their opponent was an organization large enough to govern an entire domain, after all.

It would've been one thing if they'd had a proper army, but there was no sense in asking a scant three thousand exhausted men who'd just been forced to trudge through the snow to do the impossible.

In other words, the best course of action was to retake a village near the border. That way, Archride's forces would have a strategic location from which they could send out scouting parties and gather intel. During that time, Archride was going to have to get his hands on as much booze, meat, and pleasurable company as he could to boost the soldiers' morale.

Gustav was sure to be livid if he found out they were taking such tepid-sounding measures, but trying to assault an unknown enemy encamped in a walled city of a hundred thousand with only three thousand men was suicide.

It wouldn't even be a fight.

If they wanted to wage an actual war, they needed to at least wait for Gustav's troops to join up with them. The Gustav domain's standing reserves came to roughly ten thousand. Given the Fastidious Duke's temperament, odds were that he'd bring all of them. Setting the insanity of doing so aside, wartime conscription was likely to bolster that number up to a hundred thousand. With those figures, Archride was confident the empire stood a chance against this upstart group of powerful rebels.

Until we convene with Gustav's army, we should focus on gathering as much information as possible. It's all that we should do and all that we can do. The situation was both unreasonable and unclear, so Archride knew that he needed to identify what was and wasn't within his power and order his men accordingly. Archride was a shrewd man when it came to war tactics, so much so that he was hailed as the greatest general in the northern domains.

This time, though, he was outmatched.

What he and his troops faced was already far worse than he could've ever anticipated. Archride himself realized as much when he reached the Le Luk checkpoint.

As his men braced themselves against the blizzard and trembled in fear of sudden avalanches, they finally arrived at what would've normally been a place of rest. By all accounts, the checkpoint should've provided the weary soldiers with places to put up their feet by the hearths and warm their numbed bodies with meat and drink.

When they reached the checkpoint's thirty-foot-tall gate, however, what greeted them was neither the heat of a fireplace nor the aroma of steaming food.

"Open fire!!"

Instead, they were met with two rows of gun muzzles spanning the entire width of the gate.

A maelstrom of light, sound, and metal surged forth.

"…What?"

As the noise echoed in their ears, the leading soldiers took the steel blizzard head-on. Blood sprayed through the air as they collapsed into the snow.

The bullet storm was only just getting started. A line of riflemen all pulled the bolt handles of their rifles back, ejecting the spent shells. With a push, they reloaded. After pulling the handles down to close their guns' chambers, they resumed firing.

Bolt-action rifles. To a world that knew only matchlock guns, their rate of discharge was unbelievable. The riflemen tore through the invading army's front line with ease. Archride's forces weren't just taking fire from the gate, either.

Projectiles sped from the watchtower, the windows in the walls, and even the ramparts. Barrels poked from every nook in the structure, each hurling death upon one soldier after the next.

About a week had passed since Gustav's Rage Soleil had destroyed part of Dormundt. Since then, the arms factory in Dormundt had been running day in and day out. Over three hundred members of the Order of the Seven Luminaries were now equipped with modernized gear.

Their rifles held five bullets apiece. While an imperial rifleman had to reload his barrel with gunpowder and a bullet after each shot, the Order of the Seven Luminaries soldiers could fire five times in rapid succession. In terms of raw numbers, each of them could do the shooting of a quintet of imperials. Simply put, it was like they had the bullets of fifteen hundred men bearing down on Archride's vanguard.

With the overwhelming firepower, the imperials crumpled one after another like puppets with their strings cut.

None of them screamed, for they couldn't. This wasn't how things were supposed to go. As far as any of Archride's men had known, there should've been peace and relaxation waiting for them beyond the gate.

Thoughts of safety, spirits, and sustenance had been the only thing keeping those soldiers alive during their perilous journey. Their last hopes dashed, the subjugation forces found themselves unable to process the reality unfolding before them. Their brains simply couldn't parse it, and because of that, they felt no pain.

Powerless to comprehend, those shot merely keeled over and collapsed. Their commander, Marquis Archride, was just as confused.

What's...going...on? Is that gunfire?

Archride recognized the telltale light of firearms as soldiers continued to fall one after another. They were being shot at, but why? Le Luk soldiers shouldn't have been attacking them. Archride also had to wonder what sort of armaments they were using. He'd seen a single muzzle loose multiple bullets. Nobody was reloading, nor could Archride see them adding gunpower, yet the rounds were coming ad infinitum. He'd never seen or even heard of guns like that.

Was it their enemy, then? Had the empire's mysterious foe taken over Le Luk with equally unusual weapons?

No. Impossible. Marquis Archride dismissed the thought.

Le Luk was on high alert. If there had been an emergency, they would have sent messengers to Buchwald immediately. The area's geography made pincer attacks impossible, so there was no way an enemy could've stopped the messengers.

Had there been a crisis, Archride was certain he would've heard about it.

What the hell is going—?

The colossal amount of information entering Archride's sight at once shorted out his mind. It was all too incredible to consider, and Archride stood frozen as the steel blizzard descended upon him.

"MILOOOOOORD!!"

"Ah…! Kreitzo?!"
The marquis was not pierced through, however.

A Gold Knight atop a similarly armored horse beside Archride moved to cover him with his greatshield. Hearing his subordinate's passionate cry snapped Archride back to his senses.

As the marquis gathered himself, time seemed to resume for the rest of his army, too.

"Ahhhhhhhhhhh!!!!"
"Wh-what's going on?! Why're the Le Luk guys shooting at us?!"
"Eeeeeeeek!"
The pained and confounded screams of wounded soldiers sounded from all around. Such intense cries seemed to shake the mountain itself. There was no sign of the wretched shrieks letting up, either. If anything, they only intensified with each passing second.

Formations had been broken, and the snow was stained dark with blood. Between the unexpected location of attack and its startling intensity, the vanguard had been all but annihilated.

"Milord, Le Luk must have fallen into enemy hands! Give the order to charge! They can't have more than fifty stationed at the gate! If we're prepared to make sacrifices, we can force our way through!" Kreitzo called to Marquis Archride as he held his greatshield aloft and rode.

Archride, however...

"...It's no use!"

...shouted the Gold Knight down.

Kreitzo was right—charging the gate was sure to pile on the casualties, but they could probably make it. The more significant issue was what would come afterward.

Even at a glance, Archride could see that the enemy had troops stationed over the portcullis and across the ramparts. If he and his men made it through the entrance and into the central courtyard, they'd end up taking fire from all sides. Such a short-lived victory wouldn't be worth it even if Archride's forces somehow managed not to get pinned down in the courtyard.

Le Luk had fallen into the enemy's hands.

He didn't know how they'd managed to keep messengers from reaching Buchwald, but Archride knew now that his march had been doomed since the moment the checkpoint had fallen. He had never counted on such a development. The operation's very foundations had crumbled, and building a plan atop a ruined foundation was a recipe for disaster.

Given the situation, only one option was available to the imperial forces: beating a hasty retreat.

"Kreitzo, cover me!"

"Of course!"

After giving the order to Kreitzo, Archride took a bugle off his back and blew into it with all his might.

*   *   *

BWOOOOOOOOOOOOOOOOOOOOOOOOOOOOH—

A deep sound echoed across the range.

It was just a steady stream of noise; there was nothing musical about it, but it was the known signal of retreat.

Upon hearing the horn, vanguard group members scrambled over one another as each hurried to flee faster than the other. The groups behind them, who'd more or less figured out what was going on from the screams and sounds of gunfire, turned back as well.

They were retiring without so much as trying to fight back.

"They wised up quick. That's Marquis Archride, shrewd general of the north, for you." Zest Bernard, a well-built *byuma*, leader of the Le Luk troops, and commander of the Order of the Seven Luminaries, spoke words of praise for the enemy general.

His aide-de-camp felt differently, however.

"Are you sure he isn't just a coward?"

Zest shook his head and refuted the proposition. "He's here on orders from the Fastidious Duke himself. If that guy finds out Archride gave the order to turn tail and run, he'll execute him in a heartbeat. But instead of covering his own ass, Archride made the call to keep casualties to a minimum. For him, running was a far braver choice than staying and fighting. Archride's a man who knows all too well the folly of throwing good money after bad. Honestly, I'm impressed. But even so..."

Zest paused for a moment and cast his gaze out over the scattered, fleeing imperials.

"...the reason composure's so valuable is 'cause it's so rare. There's no way any of his men keep their heads nearly so cool."

As Zest had suggested, receiving the evacuation order threw the opposing soldiers into disarray. There was a stark gap in desperation between those who'd been at the vanguard, still being shot at as they fled, and the groups behind them, whose knowledge of the situation was limited to them hearing the signal for retreat. Such a difference in circumstance created a rather disjointed rate of escape.

Frightened as they were, the vanguard group crashed into the rear guard and shoved them aside. Unfortunately, this sent the pushed people tumbling to the ground, twisting their ankles and breaking their bones. Some of the more hotheaded members of the rear guard even drew their swords and turned them on their allies.

Far more of Archride's company fell victim to disorganization and infighting than the projectiles of their actual foes. Gradually, their numbers dwindled.

If the Order of the Seven Luminaries seized upon that chaos and pressed after the escaping army, they no doubt would've crushed the imperials.

...So far, everything's going according to Mr. Tsukasa's plan.

With things proceeding as Tsukasa had described, the next course of action for the checkpoint's occupying forces was already set.

The Order of the Seven Luminaries had three hundred troops on-site. In contrast, the empire's procession alone outnumbered them more than three-to-one. With the troops waiting in Buchwald included, it was more than ten-to-one. The enemy had an overwhelming numerical advantage.

If the Seven Luminaries soldiers had a chance to reduce that wide gap in manpower, they needed to take it while they could. At the moment, the opposition was rattled and imploding from infighting. It was a perfect opportunity.

Can't say that shooting a man in the back sits great with me, but you all came storming up the mountain to try and kill us, too. Sorry, but you ain't gettin' any mercy from me.

Zest slammed a fresh clip into his rifle's depleted magazine, loading five bullets into it in a single motion.

Then he called out to those in his command.

"We're going after them. The first squadron and I will follow the enemy from behind, pursuing them down the mountain and seizing advantage of their confusion. We need to take as many of them out as we can without giving them time to regroup. Squadrons two through six on the ramparts, bring supply teams after us as quickly as possible.

If you run across any foes who've lost the will to fight, there's no need to finish them off. Just toss their weapons down the ravine and leave them for the medics. Once we all group back up, we're invading Buchwald with all we've got!

Ready? Now…move out!!"

""""Yeaaaaaaaaaaaaaaaaaaaah!!!!""""

Thus began the first significant engagement between the Order of the Seven Luminaries and the Freyjagard Empire.

Having not expected Le Luk's capture, the imperial army immediately suffered catastrophic losses and was forced to flee.

As Zest had said, Archride's decision to sound the retreat was a stellar example of Archride's wisdom and composure. However, having a thousand-man procession escape down a narrow mountain pass was easier said than done.

Their slow progress only gave rise to greater fear and confusion among the men. To make matters worse, the Order of the Seven Luminaries was bearing down on them hard and fast.

While the imperial forces tried to fight back, the raging blizzard made using their matchlock guns nigh impossible. The few shots they managed to get off didn't come anywhere close to hitting their pursuers.

Not only were the harsh winds throwing off the trajectories of their bullets, but their enemies remained beyond firing range. Archride's riflemen had an effective scope of about one hundred fifty feet. However, the two armies were over three hundred feet apart. Firearms were useless at that range, or rather, they should've been.

"How are they hitting us when we can't hit th— ARGH?!"

Deathly cries rose from the throats of those unfortunates caught at the end of the march as bullets pierced them through.

Such a development was only natural, however.

The Seven Luminaries' weapons made use of technology that the world wouldn't have otherwise seen for centuries. For one, all of their guns had rifling—spiral grooves engraved on the inside of their barrels. It gave their bullets a gyroscopic spin, decreasing their air resistance to a bare minimum. That, in turn, increased the projectiles' ballistic stability and helped prevent them from stalling. The bullets themselves were also of a wholly different shape.

The empire's soldiers' munitions were round, but the Seven Luminaries' boasted a cone shape that came to a point, like spears. It was that structure that dramatically improved their flight and precision, vastly increasing their effective range.

Zest and his people could reliably hit a target at up to a thousand feet. That was over six times what the imperial marksmen were capable of. To say that Archride's forces were outclassed was obvious. Fighting back against firepower like that was impossible, and Archride himself was well aware of how grim his situation was.

"Milord, the enemy attacks are unrelenting, and we have no way of meeting their strength! We're taking heavy losses from behind! At this rate..."

Although the panicked messenger trailed off, the implication was clear; the tail end of his company was going to be wiped out.

"...So they do mean to pursue us," Archride mumbled to himself.

Atop his horse, his face was the image of composure. He'd already gotten over the shock at having been caught up in a surprise attack. Without so much as hesitating, he issued his new orders to the runner.

"Tell those bringing up the rear that *Archride has suffered a sneak attack and died from his wounds.*"

"Wh—?!" The courier stiffened, unable to comprehend his instructions.

"That's an order. Now, go!" Archride barked at him.

"Y-yes, sir!"

Urged on, the messenger took off for the rear guard.

Gold Knight Kreitzo, visibly alarmed, rode up and took the runner's place at Marquis Archride's side.

"Milord, I must protest! If you tell them that, the chain of command will descend into chaos!" Kreitzo couldn't conceive of a reason to feed false information and sow such disorder among their own ranks. He had no idea what Archride was thinking.

The Gold Knight trusted that Archride wasn't the type of commanding officer to sacrifice his troops idly, which only deepened his confusion.

"Good," Archride replied.

"Huh?"

"With any luck, they'll throw down their arms and run for it. *And that will serve to encourage our pursuers.*"

"What do you mean?"

"We want the enemy to get overconfident, Kreitzo. They'll see our formations breaking and try to hunt down as many of us as they can. Superb as their guns are, they number only a few hundred at most.

Charging after us will sacrifice the positional advantage Le Luk offers them. That's why we need to keep giving them a reason to give chase. Once they've abandoned that high ground, we'll have a chance for a counterattack."

Having now sufficiently explained himself, Archride issued another command.

"Kreitzo, I need you to go on ahead and rendezvous with our troops in the foothills. Tell them to prepare a charge with our armored cavalry at its head. We'll whip up something too enticing for the opposition to refuse and lure them into the open plains. From there, we'll launch our charge and grind them into dust. Can I count on you?"

By feeding bad info to his troops and intentionally sending the rear guard into disarray, Archride hoped his foes would get greedy and overextend themselves. If he succeeded in drawing them into a more open area, his troops would have the advantage and could launch a counterattack that utilized the marquis's prized cavalry.

The truly wise were well aware of the fact that others were unable to keep up with their wits. Archride knew that next to none of his men would stay calm in the present situation. In a display of real prowess, he had built a plan around that fact. Archride had taken the panic of his soldiers and turned it into a key component of his strategy.

Kreitzo trembled at his own good fortune, being able to serve a man so levelheaded and sagacious.

"Of course, milord! Leave it to me!" With a confident response, Kreitzo rode off alone.

What followed played out exactly the way Archride had expected. Thanks to his misinformation, the chain of command at the rear guard collapsed.

Some of his people threw down their weapons and fled. Others surrendered to the Order of the Seven Luminaries. More still gave in to despair and mounted a futile charge. Everyone was acting independently, turning an imperial army into an unruly mob. Such a frantic crowd was no match for the forces of the Seven Luminaries.

Skirmishes broke out all over the mountain pass. In each one, the Order of the Seven Luminaries emerged victorious without a single casualty.

Dazzled by their overwhelming results, Zest and his soldiers found themselves *in the foothill plains* before they knew it.

That's when—

"All cavalry, chaaaaaaaaaaaaaarge!!!!"

"""HRAAAAAAAAAAAAAAAAAAAAAAAAGH!!!!"""
The mounted brigade that Gold Knight Kreitzo had assembled surged across the snowy grassland like a tidal wave. Altogether, there were three hundred riders. If the Order of the Seven Luminaries took such an attack head-on, they were sure to meet their end.

They had no intention of letting that happen, of course, and all fired their advanced rifles. With such mighty weapons in hand, the advancing riders must have looked like sitting ducks.

Just like how riflemen had rendered horseback riders obsolete back on Earth, the mounts collapsed helplessly under the waves of bullets, quickly becoming roadblocks for their own allies. Row after row of horses toppled over one another. In mere moments, the imperial charge had fallen to pieces.

That's how things should've played out, anyway. Reality unfolded somewhat differently. Those leading the attack were not ordinary men. They were what was referred to as armored cavalry. Both rider and steed sported heavy metal armor. The plating on a single horse alone weighed over eleven hundred pounds.

Given that they were also carrying a rider equipped with

hundred-pound armor and a greatshield, the horse's total load clocked in at nearly fifteen hundred pounds.

No average animal could've ever run while bearing such a great weight, but the empire had selectively bred unicorns so that men could ride them. Ultimately, this created a variety of magical warhorses called monoceros that were stronger than elephants and could run as fast as normal steeds even while sporting such weighty pieces of plate.

Such incredible creatures were not without drawback, however. They were incredibly expensive to maintain, to the point where only the Archride and Gustav families kept any at all. Archride only had twenty to his name. The unparalleled power they provided made such a paltry number sufficient, though.

Once the armored cavalry began their charge, nothing short of cannons or magic could stop them.

The Order of the Seven Luminaries may have sported powerful weapons, but they were still just small arms at the end of the day. Their bullets bounced off the heavy plates, leaving little more than dents and scratches.

The armored cavalry was unstoppable.

Archride was now certain of his victory, and the Order of the Seven Luminaries soldiers went pale. It wasn't because they were afraid of the overwhelming force hurtling toward them, however.

What they were afraid of—

"H-how? How is he making them dance in the palm of his hand like that?"

—was the white-haired angel boy who, three days before the battle, predicted the conflict's progression down to the letter.

Tsukasa Mikogami was the one who frightened them. Zest and his people all thought back to the briefing they'd attended a few days before.

"Listen up. When we take the enemy by surprise in Le Luk, they'll

immediately flee, right? But they won't just be making a run for it. From what I hear, the guy calling their shots is pretty crafty. Instead, they're going to try and lure us into the plains in the foothills. Then they'll use their armored cavalry to lead a big charge against us."

"Ah, so we need to make sure we don't chase them too far?"

"To the contrary. We're going to follow them there on purpose."

"Huh?"

"That armored cavalry is the only thing that poses any real danger. Foot soldiers won't be a challenge, and even mages will fall to our rifles. Those shielded mounts won't, though, making them an important source of emotional support for the enemy forces. If we leave them alive, it could cause us problems in future battles. That's why we're going to wait until the enemy is sure they've won, then crush their trump card as ostentatiously as possible. And to do that, we're going to use these."

Just as Tsukasa had instructed them, the Order of the Seven Luminaries soldiers pulled the pins of their secret weapons and tossed them at the oncoming stampede.

"Our enemy doesn't know about these yet. They'll laugh at us, thinking that we've grown desperate enough to resort to throwing stones at them."

"Ha-ha! Your bullets didn't do shit; what makes you think pebbles'll work? Dumbasses!"

"You rebels've had your fun, but it's too late to beg for your lives now!"

"Crush 'em all! Don't leave a single one alive!"

Such jeers erupted from the confident armored cavalry, yet only a moment later...

"Thus, our victory will be assured."

*   *   *

A burst of light blew the fortified horses and their riders to smithereens.

The light was followed by the noise and flame of a series of explosions. So great were the blasts that they caught unarmored members of the cavalry as well.

It hadn't been rocks that the Order of the Seven Luminaries had tossed. They'd been throwing hand grenades.

Without magic, infantry of that era wasn't supposed to be able to command such earth-shattering destruction.

The explosions eviscerated the imperial front line, and the noise sent the second line's horses into a panic, completely ruining the charge. As they were no longer in a defensive formation and weren't advancing, riders quickly became easy targets.

Waves of bullets crashed through them, shredding the mounted troops in the blink of an eye.

"………"

Partaking of the gruesome sight, Archride finally realized something; he couldn't win. He didn't know how the enemy's weapons worked. As best he could tell, the enemy infantry was equipped with firepower on par with mages or cannons.

Three thousand soldiers were nothing in the face of such might.

"…Fall back. Retreat to Dulleskoff…"

His only option was to flee once more.

Short on both men and horses, the waning subjugating army stumbled its way back to Buchwald's capital, Fortress City Dulleskoff, as fast as it could go. Numerous stragglers were abandoned along the way. Once they got to the garrison, they enacted wartime conscription, raised ten thousand new troops, and prepared to fight back a siege.

Not only did they fill every conceivable opening in the walls with sandbags, they even placed pots of water every fifty feet so they could check the ground's vibrations and make sure the enemy wasn't tunneling underneath them. The new plan was to wait inside the impregnable fortress for a few days until Gustav's army arrived.

Even with bizarre armaments, the rebels still only numbered three hundred. Storming a walled settlement was impossible with so few.

Winning may not have been an option for Archride, but he figured they'd at least be able to keep themselves alive.

Such a desperate cling to hope was quickly shattered by one of Bearabbit's cruise missiles.

The rocket soared far above Dulleskoff's walls, crashing into its tallest building, the bell tower, and blasting it to smithereens. The destruction was the Seven Luminaries' message to Archride. Dulleskoff's walls meant nothing to them.

Shortly after the explosion came an announcement via a megaphone. The Order of the Seven Luminaries demanded disarmament and unconditional surrender.

Beaten and weary, there was not a single person among the imperial force that opposed the terms.

With that, the Seven Luminaries took Dulleskoff and captured Marquises Buchwald and Archride. In practice, that meant that two more northern domains were under their control, and it had only been a single short week since the opening of hostilities in the Le Luk mountains.

While the subjugating army had been reduced to less than five hundred men, the Order of the Seven Luminaries suffered a mere four injuries. One man tripped and fractured a bone while descending the mountains. The other three were those he fell into as he stumbled.

Meanwhile, in Gustav, the domain's full army was still in Millevana, the domain's capital and the city that housed the Office of the Warden of the North. It was supposed to have been heading to rendezvous with Archride's forces yet remained curiously stationary.

One had to wonder why, and the answer to that question could be found in the smoke billowing up from Millevana. At the center of the city, the Office of the Warden of the North was burning.

As the subjugating army and the Order of the Seven Luminaries clashed, another war was beginning over in the Gustav domain.

All over the city, Gustav's army was fighting against a force that called themselves the Blue Brigade.

Gustav's mad glorification of the emperor had destroyed the domain's economy all to construct a few gold statues and beautify his lands. Out of concern for the affected peasants, a group of Gustav domain nobles had banded together and risen up against him.

"Weed out those traitors infesting the Findolph domain."

After gathering in Millevana in accordance with Gustav's order, they rose the banner of revolt and turned against their lord.

Rage Soleil, Gustav's trump card, had been the Blue Brigade's biggest obstacle. After he'd expended it on the Seven Luminaries, the Blue Brigade had quickly found themselves with an excuse to assemble their full forces at Gustav's front gate.

It was the best opportunity they could've asked for.

Of the ten thousand troops Gustav amassed in Millevana, all seven thousand soldiers not under his direct command turned on him. With such overwhelming numbers and surprise on their side, the Blue Brigade surrounded the warden's office in no time.

Gustav's army responded by moving their defensive line back into the warden's office and holing up there. The structure doubled as a fortress and was fully equipped with pitfall traps, secret passages, and clockwise spiral staircases designed to hinder the sword arms of any climbing up. Such an advantageous position should've allowed Gustav's people to repel the intruders. Much to their surprise, things did not go well for them, however.

The Blue Brigade had an ace up their sleeve—prodigy journalist Shinobu Sarutobi. Before the battle, she'd pilfered the structure's architectural plan and told the Blue Brigade where all the traps and secret passages were.

In the end, every trip wire and pitfall was rendered worthless, and the hidden corridors only served to offer the Blue Brigade more avenues of ingress.

Unable to hold their position, the defenders' line steadily crumbled, and Gustav's army was routed.

Meanwhile, Shinobu Sarutobi and the Blue Brigade redheaded knight Jeanne du Leblanc took advantage of the chaos to press deep into the fortress and corner Gustav in one of its towers. It was only when the two women reached the top of the tower that they finally met the Fastidious Duke face-to-face.

When Gustav saw that one of them was an Imperial Silver Knight, his black eyes flared up with fury.

"As one of His Grace's knights, you would bare your fangs against the empire?!"

Jeanne responded by leveling her blood-soaked sword at him.

"A nation's foundation is its people. Without them, it's nothing. Any noble who dares tyrannize them is the true traitor. As I understand, Duke Gustav, you yourself once said those very words."

"...!"

"If you have even a shred of sense left in you, surrender now and retain your dignity as a loyal retainer!"

"I see. So Blumheart's the mastermind. That man refuses to wake from his idealistic dreams, and now he's gone and dragged other aristocrats into his foolery, too!" As he spat those words, fire erupted from the stumps where Gustav's arms had once been.

They burned hot enough to melt Gustav's tunic, writhing like they had minds of their own and molding themselves into the shape of arms. The molded flames grabbed a sword hanging from the wall and held it at the ready.

"I, Gustav, will sear away that moronic illusion, along with your lives!"

"If you won't surrender, you leave us no choice! Let's go, Shinobu!" Jeanne declared.

"You got it!" Shinobu replied.

The pair split up, each running toward one of Gustav's flanks. In response, the duke materialized six burning spheres around himself.

"Firebolt!!"

Gustav sent three of the flaming balls at each of his opponents. While the conjured missiles were fast, they could still be followed by the eye. With their superb reflexes, both Jeanne and Shinobu deftly avoided the oncoming magical attacks.

Instead of stopping, the molten spheres just crashed into the spire's walls and exploded. They blasted all the way through the stone, exposing the interior of the tower to the open air.

It was like they were being bombarded by cannon fire; Jeanne and Shinobu were done for.

While his opponents were preoccupied with avoiding his first move, Gustav summoned up another set of fireballs.

This mage nonsense is getting real old real fast...! Shinobu thought.

It was like fighting against an enemy with a rapid-fire grenade launcher. Such strength made it no surprise to learn that mages were extremely well regarded in a world where traditional firepower topped out at crossbows and matchlock guns.

With things proceeding as they were, Shinobu knew that she and Jeanne wouldn't be able to get in close. On the other hand, continuing to dodge was problematic in and of itself.

If Gustav kept lashing out with such devastating magic, the tower was liable to collapse. Jeanne and Shinobu had gone in knowing that their foe was a powerful mage, however. They most assuredly hadn't barged in without a plan.

Shinobu pulled a yellow, ping-pong-ball-sized sphere from her pocket. "Jeanne, *cover your eyes!*" After shouting out the prearranged warning, Shinobu threw the little object at her feet.

A surge of white light flooded the room to the point where nothing else was visible. It was one of Shinobu's ninja tools—a flash grenade. Gustav, who hadn't shielded himself, was immediately overwhelmed.

"GRAAAGH! MY EEEEEYES!"

The temporary blindness threw him off guard, and the fireballs floating around him vanished. Jeanne took advantage of that opening to close the gap, bringing her sword down toward the duke's neck.

"Traitorous Gustav, your head will roll!"

However...

"Hwuh?!"

Right when it seemed the finishing blow had been struck, something unbelievable happened.

Gustav, who should've been blinded, blocked Jeanne's attack. In fact, he did more than just that.

"A lowly Silver like you can never measure up to a Platinum Knight!!!!"

He even managed a counterattack with a swing of his sword and blazing arms—a powerful, practiced, two-hit combo. The first strike came from above, forcing Jeanne to stiffen her guard. The second came from below, knocking her sword upward.

"Gweh?!"

Finally, Gustav sank a kick into Jeanne's exposed abdomen and sent her flying several feet backward.

Having dealt with Jeanne, Gustav turned his still-sightless eyes toward Shinobu. The ninja clutched a kunai in each hand and was trying to charge at the man from behind.

"Kraaaaaaaah!!"

The duke curled a free flame-hand into a fist and swung it straight at her. As the burning limb hurled itself forward, it expanded to a massive size and took on the shape of a gaping dragon's maw.

Yikes! Shinobu threw herself to the side, too desperate to figure out how she was going to land. She managed to barely avoid the scorching dragon head but could smell the tips of her hair cooking.

Gustav's attacks had been right on the money, and they forced the ninja-journalist to wonder if perhaps her flash grenade hadn't worked. The duke clearly didn't move like a blind man. If he really could see, that meant big trouble for Shinobu and Jeanne.

Shinobu's narrow dodge had completely thrown off her balance, and she was tumbling toward the ground in a very bad position. Unless she did something, she was going to land directly on her right shoulder. If Gustav launched another attack while she was in such a position, that'd be the end of the line.

Faced with a difficult choice, Shinobu made a split-second decision. As she crashed onto the ground, she hurled the kunai in her left hand. The idea was to create a diversion. With any luck, Gustav would try to defend himself, which would slow down his follow-up strike just long enough for Shinobu to get back on her feet.

Much to the Prodigy's surprise, however...

"Nragh?!"

The kunai sped through the air undetected and dug into the Fastidious Duke's thigh.

"Huh?!"

As Shinobu lay on the ground, a wave of confusion washed over her. *That was too easy*, she thought.

Gustav hadn't even tried to dodge or guard himself. Then Shinobu was struck by the notion that perhaps he hadn't ignored her kunai, but rather, he hadn't *seen* it.

Wait, is he sensing our positions with heat or something?! Betting on her hunch, Shinobu made her move. The moment she got up, she threw her other kunai. Her target wasn't Gustav himself this time; it was what was hanging over his head.

A chandelier hung suspended in the room by a chain.

"GAAAAAAAAAAAH!!!!"

The kunai did its job, severing the chain and dropping the chandelier directly onto Gustav.

The Blue Brigade's sudden attack had left the duke without enough time to light the swinging candelabra's candles, and just as Shinobu had thought, he was using heat to supplement his lost vision. Unaware of what had been cut free above him, Gustav was promptly crushed by the chandelier as it crashed to the floor.

Ornate glass and metal stylings became as knives that stabbed into Gustav's body. A pool of blood began to spread beneath his crumpled form.

"You killed him?!" Jeanne exclaimed.

"Don't jinx it...," Shinobu replied. Indeed, the duke still drew breath, bashed and bloodied though he was.

"Damn youuuuu...! You worms who would defy His Grace are

crafty, I'll give you that! But don't go thinking you've defeated the mighty Gustav so easily!"

A furious bellow echoed out from beneath the ruined fixture. As Gustav's rage reached its climax, patterns of light began flowing out from below the chandelier and filling the room. With a flash, they shifted from red to white, swelling in heat and intensity—

Hoo boy, that looks like bad news. Shinobu's *kunoichi* sixth sense was tingling.

"Jeanne!"

"Huh?!"

Choosing to trust her intuition, Shinobu dashed toward Jeanne at full speed.

After ramming straight into the other woman, Shinobu kept running. Her legs carried both of them outside through one of the holes Gustav had blown in the walls. Then she adeptly wrapped her scarf around her hands and feet, unfurling it into a parachute.

"Grab on!" Shinobu shouted to Jeanne, whom she'd essentially just thrown off a tower.

Unsurprisingly startled, Jeanne still reacted swiftly enough all the same.

"Got it!" Jeanne drew the whip hanging from her waist, then hurled the length of it into the air and wrapped it around Shinobu's torso.

No sooner had she done so than—

—the tower Gustav was in exploded. Its masonry was devoured by a scorching white light.

The explosion wasn't sated with just the spire, either. A chain of secondary bursts went off as well, eventually demolishing the entire Office of the Warden of the North.

©Sacrane

As the shock wave sent Shinobu spinning about in the air, the scene below them took Jeanne's breath away.

"Wh-what is this…?"

"Looks like he prolly planted bombs throughout the building in case anything ever happened. Could just be magic, though."

"Y-you have my thanks, Shinobu. If not for you, I'd have been caught up in the blast. And good work, sensing that danger…!"

"Hee-hee. Danger-sensing's a must-have skill for any good risk-takin' journalist!"

It had all started the day Shinobu began elementary school. A bow trap aimed right at her temple had greeted her when she came home and opened the door, marking the first in a long line of brutal training techniques. "Domestic violence" didn't even begin to describe it. If she'd let up her guard for even a moment, day or night, she would've died. Spending a decade in an environment like that would've taught anyone a thing or two about perceiving threats.

Eventually, as the shock waves died down and the two of them began gently descending, three ally dragoons—knights mounted on small flying dragons—flew over to them. It was the survivors from the Blue Brigade's small air force, and they were quite clearly overjoyed that Jeanne and Shinobu were safe.

"Hey, Jeanne, you're all right!" one fighter exclaimed.

"Yes, but only thanks to Shinobu!" she replied.

"Y'know, that's some impressive stuff! I've been doing this soldier thing for a while now, but this is the first time I've ever seen someone fly like a dragoon without needing a dragon!"

"Hee-hee, go on, praise me more!" Shinobu said gleefully.

"So, Jeanne, what happened to old Gustav?" inquired a dragoon.

"He was at the center of the explosion. I can't imagine he survived."

"Well now, that's some good news if ever I heard any! I'm going to head back and report to Count Blumheart at once!"

"I'll leave that to you, then. The two of us will float down and join up with you later," Jeanne decided.

"Got it! See you then!"

After exchanging pleasantries, the dragoons headed back to the main Blue Brigade camp.

Jeanne watched them go, then returned her gaze to the burning structure below. "...Still, what kind of man blows himself up along with his castle?" she muttered.

"That old guy didn't give a crap about anyone's life, not even his own. He was probably happy getting a chance to sacrifice himself for the empire," Shinobu reasoned.

"A nation owes everything to the value its people create. Survival of the fittest might be the national policy, but any country that abandons its people has no future. With this, the Gustav domain is saved. All that's left is to take the gold Gustav gathered and use it to improve the lives of the citizens as quickly as possible."

Easier said than done, if y'ask meee... Although she didn't voice them, Shinobu had her doubts.

Jeanne's chivalrous desire to protect the weak was genuine. After spending the past few days with her, Shinobu was sure enough of that. Count Blumheart, the leader of the Blue Brigade that Jeanne herself held in high esteem, may very well have been cut from the same cloth.

From what Shinobu had heard, he'd expressed misgivings about Gustav's statesmanship from an early stage. Even after Gustav outranked him, Blumheart still used their shared childhood at the imperial military academy as means for an audience in order to warn the Fastidious Duke not to ignore his subjects' well-being. Annoyed, Gustav had banished him to the domain's outskirts for his troubles.

From there, Blumheart had gathered Jeanne and other such good-hearted individuals together and formed the beginnings of what would become the Blue Brigade.

However, what had their organization become?

As Gustav's leadership worsened, the Blue Brigade had grown larger and larger. Unfortunately, many of the group's nobles had only joined after the negative effects from Gustav's policies started impacting them personally.

Shinobu believed it unlikely that such people would be eager to help those in need. More concerning, however, was Shinobu's hunch that Gustav wasn't actually dead yet. She thought back to what the madman said right before he'd done himself in.

The duke hadn't spoken with the tone of a man prepared to accept his fate, and that fact weighed heavily on Shinobu's mind. Her suspicions only deepened when no corpse was found in the wreckage.

Gustav's explosion had succeeded in taking out fifteen hundred soldiers in an instant, though—enemies and allies alike. Deciding that it didn't make sense for the man at the epicenter of such a blast to come out in one piece, the nobles soon made the decision to call off the search.

Word began to travel that Oslo el Gustav had blown himself to smithereens, and the Blue Brigade was declared victorious.

In place of Count Blumheart, who had tragically died during the final battle, Marquis Conrad took over as temporary lord of the domain, drawing a final curtain on the war.

CHAPTER 1

❦ The Blue Brigade ❦

After the battle between the Seven Luminaries and the imperial subjugating army, talk about the Seven Luminaries monopolized conversations across the Archride and Buchwald domains. One couldn't pass a street corner, worksite, or tavern without hearing about them.

Everyone was talking about the group from the north that had come bearing an "equality for all" style of rule. Gossip about how the rebels were poised to overthrow the feudal system ran rampant.

"Hard to believe, huh. Findolph and Buchwald are one thing, but they even took down Archride like it was nothing."

"Did he not send out his armored cavalry or something?"

"That's just it—a soldier buddy of mine told me that they all mobilized...and got completely wiped out."

"The invincible armored cavalry *lost*?! They said the Yamato samurai could cut through steel, and even they were no match for the armored cavalry!"

"Word is, when the armored cavalry charged their infantry, the ground exploded under their feet. It was like cannon fire came outta nowhere."

"I heard the Seven Luminaries' God can grant magical powers to normal old schmucks. That's why all their soldiers can do crazy shit like that. They're all basically mages. Marquis Archride made the right call surrendering. I mean, they've got a real deity on their side. There's no way some average guy could overcome a ten-to-one numbers advantage and take over two imperial domains in a week."

"Well, looks like things worked out pretty good for us little guys."

Everyone nodded in agreement.

The commoners had initially been hesitant about being taken over by some strange religious group. However, when they experienced the benevolent governing of the Seven Luminaries firsthand and saw how they were working to round up corrupt nobles, few were eager to voice complaints. For the first time in many years, there was hope.

Some truly began to believe the world was actually changing. The prospect was so exciting it made their hearts throb.

"You hear what happened to Baron Zamud's asshole son?"

"That guy who was going and prostrating himself in front of all the people he'd used his dad's power to abuse, you mean? They say he was paying them off not to rat him out."

"Well, apparently someone spilled the beans, and he ended up getting arrested."

"I mean, the asshole executed a couple of people. Didn't even give 'em trials. No wonder someone was fed up with his shit."

"When they dragged him off, he was shouting 'I don't want to die' with snot dripping down his face and piss spilling down his pants."

"Ha-ha, serves him right."

"Man, I still can't believe it. Nobles getting locked up for hurting us commoners…"

"Yeah, and it's all thanks to the Seven Luminaries."

"I know the emperor won't go down without a fight, but I hope they beat him."

Poorer folk weren't the only ones who felt a new era creeping up along the horizon, either.

The nobles sensed it, too.

A week after the annexation, the Seven Luminaries took their detained lords, Buchwald and Archride, to the Manufacturing District they'd build around the thermal power station beside Dormundt.

The goal of their little field trip was to set Buchwald and Archride at ease.

The Seven Luminaries had annexed Buchwald's and Archride's domains by defeating their joint military forces, but they didn't have the manpower to hold them, in truth. Compared to the Findolph domain, which boasted less than a century's worth of cultivation, each of them had far more people and land.

If the Seven Luminaries were going to retain dominion over both domains, assistance from its current ruling class would be essential. Thus, the decision was made to show Buchwald and Archride just how powerful the Order of the Seven Luminaries was. In doing so, the hope was to cut out their animosity at the root and secure their cooperation.

It perhaps went without saying, but to the two lords, their tour was just one world-shattering surprise after another.

"Th-this…is this really rifling?! Like the imperial workshops' latest!"

Upon being shown the arms factory, Archride let out an awe-struck yelp.

Their guide, Dormundt's former mayor and current minister of the Findolph province, Walter von Heiseraat, seemed impressed. "Sixty years old and still leading the charge. I should have known you'd recognize what this is, Marquis Archride."

"...I'd heard reports, but this is my first time actually seeing it in the flesh."

"U-um, Marquis Archride, if I may... What exactly is 'rifling'?"

Marquis Buchwald, a short, timid-looking middle-aged man, asked nervously for an explanation, to which Archride showed him the gun's opening and spoke.

"Rifling is a technique where you carve spiral grooves inside a gun barrel. By causing your bullets to spin, you make them fly farther and straighter. The imperial workshops came up with the idea about a year ago, but it was difficult and costly to implement, so they halted development so they could focus on upgrading the army from matchlock to flintlock guns instead." As he spoke, Archride cast his gaze around the factory in disbelief. All around him, *hyuma* and *byuma* were using machines he'd never seen before to construct gun parts in rapid succession.

"So this is where you're mass-producing guns that even the empire couldn't create?" he inquired.

"That it is. The Order of the Seven Luminaries is equipped with five hundred such rifles at the moment, but that number is rising as we speak. Eventually, we plan to have our entire army equipped with them," Heiseraat explained.

"The level of output here is remarkable..."

"It's all thanks to the facilities granted to us by God Akatsuki of the Seven Luminaries. The various tools move on their own through divine 'electricity' magic, allowing us to produce intricate parts with ease."

"...It's true, even the speed you're producing the barrels at is unprecedented..."

This world had yet to develop the capability to carve out a metal bar's insides via drill. For them to construct a hollow metal tube, they needed to take iron plates and round them around a mold.

Even just producing a single matchlock gun necessitated the forging of iron plates, tempering them around a cylindrical core called a mandrel to shape the barrel, coating them in a layer of steel, and then tempering them again. The mere thought of the process was exhausting.

In the Seven Luminaries' factory, however, all they had to do to make a barrel was run a gun drill attached to a lathe through a round steel bar.

Just that single process made a remarkable difference in terms of the speed of production.

"…Well, I suppose that solves the mystery of how you all had so many guns and how they shot so far. Nevertheless, there's still something I'm curious about—that rapid-fire. Was that more divine providence?" Dizzy as he was at the alien level of technical prowess on display, Archride asked another question.

Heiseraat responded by beckoning him and Buchwald over into another Manufacturing District area, a shooting range for the finished guns. From there, he picked a golden piece of metal up off the table and showed it to his guests.

"The key to that rapid-fire is these."

Archride cocked his head to the side. "What are they? Thorns? Arrowheads?"

"These are the bullets we use in the guns," Heiseraat revealed.

"Bullets?! That enormous metal spike is a bullet?!"

"It is indeed. Well, I suppose technically only the off-color part on the end is."

"Just the tip? Then, what's the fat section on the bottom?" Buchwald asked, finally piping up.

"You raise an excellent question, Marquis Buchwald. For therein lies the secret behind the rapid-fire."

Heiseraat picked up a rifle lying against the shooting range's wall.

"The inside of the bigger part is hollow, and it's filled with *a certain something*. Marquis Archride, care to take a stab at what that something might be?" As he elaborated, Heiseraat loaded a five-round magazine into the gun.

Archride paused and thought for a moment, but there was only one thing that made sense to load in with munitions, and he quickly arrived at the answer.

"Could it really be...gunpowder?!"

Heiseraat fired a shot at one of the range's targets.

"Precisely. Unlike the firearms we've used up until now, where we had to load the bullet and the gunpowder separately, these weapons combine them and, in doing so, combine all the steps of reloading into one. Then, if we combine that concept with a series of spring-based mechanisms..."

With a practiced hand, Heiseraat operated the bolt-action rifle while giving his explanation. First, he pulled the bolt handle down, then back. That made the gun's internal spring push the magazine's next bullet up, the pressure from which caused the spent shell to eject. Then he loaded the raised bullet into the chamber by returning the bolt handle to its starting position. Finally, after he raised the lever and sealed the chamber—

"...We can load the shots in ahead of time and fire them off one after another."

—he fired a series of bullets off in rapid succession by repeating the same motions.

Five shots in a row.

The two marquises trembled as they looked on in shock.

"How utterly brilliant..."

They were partially shaking with fear at how advanced their former foes' technology was, but more than that, they were awestruck at the sheer ingenuity that went into every aspect of the rifle's construction. Projectiles and propellant were packaged together and then loaded in sequence via springs.

It was so simple that Archride and Buchwald could picture it in their heads. That's what made it all so impressive.

"H-hold on a minute, now!" Knowing how the Seven Luminaries' guns worked made Marquis Buchwald all the more confused, however. "These use gunpowder to fire off bullets, just like the empire's?!"

"That's right," answered Heiseraat.

"But that doesn't make sense! Your people must've fired off thousands of shots in that last battle! Where did all that gunpowder come from?!"

Marquis Archride took over from there, saying, "He's right; that is strange. Findolph never seemed too excited about arming his men with firearms, and I'd heard that the city watch in your old post, Dormundt, had only a few guns to go around. How did you get gunpowder in such quantities? Saltpeter, the raw material, is hardly easy to come by."

"Heh. That one you'll have to chalk up to a divine miracle," Heiseraat asserted.

"A miracle?" Archride asked.

Heiseraat nodded in reply.

"The thing is, I found it just as curious as you two did. The angel who built these facilities has a retainer, a metal spider called Bearabbit. He's the one that taught us how to build guns, and I asked him where the gunpowder came from. I could hardly believe it myself when I heard the answer.

"Through the power of a divine miracle...in essence, by magic, they created gunpowder from thin air."

"Th-thin air?!" Buchwald exclaimed.

"You mean to say they whipped up such a precious resource from nothing at all?! Is that even possible...?" Archride asked, dubious.

"Apparently so, if they use a divine spell called 'Haber-Bosch process.'"

In truth, the "Haber-Bosch process" Heiseraat was referring to wasn't a supernatural marvel at all. An assumption that it was had been the natural conclusion for someone unfamiliar with the method, though.

After all, neither Bearabbit nor his genius inventor, Ringo Oohoshi, were mages of any sort.

However, the process in question had revolutionized human history to such an extent that calling it *magic* wasn't far off the mark.

Put simply, the Haber-Bosch process used heat and pressure to cause a chemical reaction that used iron oxide as a catalyst to pull nitrogen from the air and make it into ammonia.

Back at the start of the 1900s when it was first developed on Earth, humanity used it to get the nitrogen they needed for their crops from the atmosphere in the form of nitrogenous fertilizer. Doing so vastly increased the amount of food they were able to produce from a given plot, causing a record-breaking population boom. Due to its outstanding results, the Haber-Bosch process came to be known as "the magic that turns water, coal, and air into bread."

Unfortunately, the boons borne from revolutionary technologies aren't always positive. The Haber-Bosch process brought calamity down on mankind, as well. Fertilizer wasn't the only thing that could be made from ammonia. Gunpowder could be made from it, too.

Ammonia was required to synthesize saltpeter, also known as potassium nitrate, the raw ingredient behind gunpowder. With ammonia suddenly cheap and easy to obtain, saltpeter became more available than ever before. Countries all over the planet rapidly modernized their armies. Many believed this rapid upgrade in firearms to be one of the significant inciting incidents to World War I. That was the kind of malignant technology the Order of the Seven Luminaries was using.

Through it, they'd been able to obtain the gunpowder necessary to upgrade their army from seemingly nothing. Such a process had proven impossible to plainly explain to this world's locals, however.

When Heiseraat had come asking Bearabbit about the gunpowder manufacturing, Bearabbit had given him a thorough explanation about fixing nitrogen with an iron oxide catalyst, but the only response he'd gotten back was a blank stare. No one here knew what the air they so nonchalantly breathed was composed of, after all. It was unlikely they realized it was made of anything at all.

In the end, Bearabbit had said, "*Well, just think of it as divine magic that makes it pawsible to pull gunpowder out of the air.*"

Basically, he'd given up on explaining it. Sometimes, even AI felt like passing the buck. Such a simple answer was not without some portion of truth, though.

After all, the people of this world had no idea that the atmosphere was composed of elements like nitrogen. As far as they were concerned, the Haber-Bosch process really was a miracle that made gunpowder from nothing.

"You were standing on the front lines, Marquis Archride, so you of all people should realize that nothing short of divine providence could've created the amount of gunpowder the Order of the Seven Luminaries used in that battle."

"Th-that's…" A bead of sweat formed on Archride's forehead. He couldn't refute it. To him, conjuring up the substance was more believable than somehow managing to import a huge quantity of it.

Nothing short of a godly phenomenon could have been ascribed to such a marvel.

"It all just seems so unreal…"

When at last Archride and Buchwald accepted the truth of the matter, their faces grew even paler. Having seen the Seven Luminaries' factory firsthand, they could tell that these weren't just some rebellious upstarts equipped with fancy guns. The enemy that had so thoroughly routed them was an organization equipped with something far more terrifying than guns—knowledge.

Who...who in the world are these boys and girls calling themselves gods and angels?! Is one of them truly an awesome deity from above? Although he hated to admit it, Archride did have to consider the possibility. He then shook his head to dismiss the thought. Surely it was impossible.

God doesn't exist, Archride told himself. If he did, there was no way the religious persecution the empire had once carried out would've gone as smoothly as it had. Archride knew his history. He didn't believe in heavenly powers or the omnipotence thereof.

Little did he know how difficult doubting was about to become.

"Have a look, Marquis Archride."

Heiseraat took a pile of papers tied together with a string and handed them to him.

"Hmm? What's this?"

"The Order of the Seven Luminaries' commander and his men were given this battle plan just before we engaged your army. Mr. Tsukasa, the angel serving as our new God's tactician, told me to show this to you. He assured me that it would help convince you."

Confused, Archride received the report and quickly scanned it.

"..." The man's face went a shade paler than it had when he'd seen the rifling or learned of the miraculous Haber-Bosch process.

From the moment they set foot on Le Luk to when they'd laid down their arms at Dulleskoff, every action his army had taken was laid out nigh prophetically in the battle plan.

"Ha... Ha-ha..."

Archride couldn't help but let out a dry chuckle.

What a world...

If the written account had only contained the orders he'd actually given, Marquis Archride could've dismissed it as something the Seven Luminaries had prepared after the fact to trick him. Included in the documents were not only the list of orders he'd issued, but also detailed alternate courses that Archride had considered in each moment. These were plans he'd contemplated but never issued.

From there, the papers became a detailed flowchart with paths for each possibility, allowing those who read it to respond to whatever choices Archride might have made.

Given that Archride himself was the one who'd considered all the various options and possibilities listed on the chart, he knew it impossible to deny the accuracy of the documents. The man knew why Tsukasa Mikogami had deigned to show this report to him.

Tsukasa was sending him a message.

"No matter what you did, you would still have been dancing on the palm of my hand."

Faced with such a revelation, what other option was there but to laugh?

"Ha-ha-ha-ha-ha!"

"M-Marquis Archride?" Buchwald asked.

"I see, I see. So we were doomed from the start. Buchwald, my man...it seems we really did go to war against gods."

Archride was certain now. This was the work of no mortal. No human could've possibly accomplished this much. He was completely outmatched in both strategy and perspective. Engaging in a battle against people who could create such a report was nothing more than base folly.

It was within that moment that the last scraps of Archride's loyalty to the empire, and his desire to fight back, vanished all at once. He turned to Heiseraat and promptly swore fealty to the Seven Luminaries.

"We cannot defeat the divine. The Archride domain hereby pledges allegiance to the Seven Luminaries."

Once Archride had finished, Marquis Buchwald pledged allegiance to the Seven Luminaries in turn. He'd long been Archride's flunky. Following him was the only way Buchwald knew how to live.

Thus, the Seven Luminaries solidified their standing in the Buchwald and Archride domains. Through the generous cooperation of each domain's lord, they were able to carry out their reforms to bring equality to all.

Curiously, the leaders of the Order of the Seven Luminaries, the High School Prodigies, were nowhere to be found in Dormundt. They weren't in Buchwald or Archride, either.

They were staying in the Gustav domain, as guests of the Blue Brigade.

"Ahh… This is exquisite…"

"…It feels like I'm lying in a field of flowers, that it does."

A villa by the name of Nord sat nestled in the Gustav domain. It was a luxurious palace that had been built to accommodate inspectors from the imperial capital and was generally only used on such occasions. After the Blue Brigade took control of the domain, they gave the High School Prodigies a special invitation to partake of its hospitalities.

One such amenity was the aromatherapy massages that the group's female members were in the middle of sampling.

Prodigy journalist Shinobu Sarutobi, whom the Blue Brigade had mistaken as a Yamato survivor, had fought alongside them on the front lines. Now, she and the other girls were relaxing in ecstasy, surrounded by the smell of roses as a group of maids masterfully rubbed and kneaded the slopes and valleys of their bodies.

"Word is, these are the oils the empress herself uses. You can't find them for sale anywhere, so they had to send out for 'em special just so we could get the royal treatment. Sweet, huh?" Shinobu said with a grin.

"That's right, ma'am. Imperial mages use spirits to draw out the active ingredients, making them much purer than the kinds you can get by distillation or compression. My master, Marquis Conrad, will be overjoyed to hear that they're to your liking," replied an attendant.

"Pretty nice of them to use something so valuable on just us ladies. Feels like we hit the jackpot, huh, Ringo?"

As she lay facedown to receive her massage, Shinobu chatted up the petite girl sitting on the next bed over who was getting an arm rub—Ringo Oohoshi, the genius inventor.

However—

"Uh-huh…"

—Ringo barely gave any reply.

"Hey, what's up? You feelin' sick?" Shinobu asked.

"Oh? Are you unwell, Ringo?" Keine Kanzaki added.

Having now worried the Prodigies' doctor, Ringo hurriedly shook her head in the negative. With a thin, faltering voice, she explained, "It just…seems…like a waste…to use something so pricey…on me…"

"Huh? Why's that?" Shinobu sounded puzzled.

"I—I mean…I'm not…as pretty as the rest of you…and it's not like I have…a great body, either…"

As she spoke, Ringo glanced at the other two as well as Aoi Ichijou, the master swordswoman.

Aoi had long, slender legs and a tight, trim waist. Shinobu was on the shorter end, but she had a lively, feminine figure. Despite Keine's boobs each being nearly as big as Ringo's head, they were perky and didn't sag in the slightest.

All three of them had such attractive physiques that even though she was a girl, Ringo found her eyes drawn to them. She looked down at her own body, comparing it to the others'.

Her arms and legs were small and short like a child's, and her breasts were barely even large enough to identify her as a female. Ringo's figure couldn't have been further from an hourglass shape. Realizing just how inadequately she stacked up, the inventor let out a sigh.

Just as Ringo was sinking into a funk, however—

"What're you taaaaaalking about? These silky-smooth cheeks are worth the price of admission alone!"

"Hwa-wa?!"

—Shinobu leaped up from her bed, wrapped Ringo in a big hug, and nuzzled her cheek.

"When it comes to cuteness, you're a chart-topper, Ringo. I meet a lot of entertainment industry folks in my line of work, and hardly any of them come *close* to being as cute as you."

"That's quite right. Besides, having a nice figure isn't the only way for a woman to be appealing. I don't think it's a waste at all," Keine commented.

"Indeed. Ringo, m'lady, I find you downright adorable, that I do… In fact, given my unfeminine height, I daresay I find myself a bit jealous." Aoi was similarly quick to chime in.

"And y'know, even back on Earth, you were actually more popular than most idols," Shinobu remarked.

"N-no way," Ringo whispered.

©Sacraneco

"Yes way. Heck, not only did you have a dedicated thread on 2chan's Academia: Science board, it filled up like five hundred times! Plus, whenever a science journal wrote an article about you, it would sell a hundred times more copies than the other ones!"

"?!"

Hearing Shinobu tell her that struck Ringo speechless. Ringo had previously lived in outer space and had relegated most of her communication with the outside world to Bearabbit. This was the first she'd learned of any of this.

"Plus, having a nice body's all about the effort you put in. Us women keep growing until we're in our twenties, and if you just want bigger knockers, there's plenty of techniques to get you there. Wanna try out the ol' boob-enhancing massage that's been passed down in my family for generations?" asked Shinobu.

"Oh? This technique of yours, does it actually exist?" The proposition had piqued Ringo's interest.

"Hey, having decent tits is one of the surest ways to get guys wrapped around your little finger. It's a pretty important skill to have for a *kunoichi* like me." As Shinobu spoke, she jiggled her own breasts.

Seeing them bounce made Ringo wonder if hers would be like that after receiving this mysterious massage.

"Well? Wanna try? I will warn you, it'll tickle a bit at first," Shinobu offered yet again.

"Um…"

Ringo's gaze darted around. Her discomfort with social situations made the prospect of being seen naked all the more embarrassing. At the same time, however, she also remembered how she'd felt after seeing Tsukasa sleeping with his head on Lyrule's lap.

Ringo didn't want to lose. The genius inventor knew she was no match for Lyrule when it came to femininity, yet her resolve remained unshaken.

She refused to give up on the feelings she'd been harboring since that incident back in middle school. If Shinobu's method could even make her the tiniest bit more shapely, Ringo was willing to try it.

"...Y-yes, please..." Ringo's face flushed apple-red as she accepted Shinobu's proposal.

Shinobu, more than happy to oblige, took over for Ringo's maid.

One of the maids, who'd been glancing over and watching the scene play out, turned to the *fifth High School Prodigy present*.

"And you, Ms. Akatsuki? Would you like to try the empire's famous breast-enhancing massage?"

"I'M GOOD, THANKS!"

The Prodigies' brilliant magician, Prince Akatsuki, was lying sprawled atop a bed, covered by a single loincloth and receiving the same aromatherapy massage as the girls.

Then, still covering his eyes with his hands so as not to see the girls in their immodest states of undress, he let out a pained groan. "Man, why does this always happen to meeeee...?"

One had to wonder why Akatsuki, a boy, was there at all. The culprit was his own appearance. The diminutive blond was very pretty. His petite build didn't give away his gender, and often, the people he met would regularly mistake him for a girl.

The maids of Nord, having been no exception, had carted him off with the women. Despite Akatsuki's loud protestations, Shinobu had cut him off before the magician had ever had the chance to get the words out.

"Akatsuki, don't. If you tell the maids off, they might get executed. Just give up and go along with it."

Akatsuki knew all too well just how cheap some lives were considered to be in the world they were in, so he knew Shinobu wasn't joking. He wasn't about to make a fuss if someone's life was on the line. Unfortunately, his silence meant he'd been dragged along with the girls to their aromatherapy massage.

With his hands clamped over his eyes, Akatsuki prayed desperately for the whole thing to end as quickly as possible. The self-imposed blindness only made his reactions to tactile stimuli on his skin all the more intense, however.

"Ah—"

A maid's oiled hand traveled gently over the bumps in his rib cage and sent a shiver down his spine. A slight noise escaped Akatsuki's mouth. Hearing it, the attending woman looked down at him and smiled cheerfully.

"Hmm-hmm, Ms. Akatsuki, your skin is so sensitive. And it's so clear, and white, and youthful... I'm sure that gentlemen must find it very attractive."

"WHYYYYYYY MEEEEEEEE?!"

Out of all the accolades the magician had received in his seventeen years of life, he had never been more displeased to be complimented.

Elsewhere, the boys-minus-Akatsuki were taking a dip in the palace's grand bath, their unmentionables covered by loincloths.

Shrewd businessman Masato Sanada rubbed his stuffed belly, then turned to his tub mate, Tsukasa.

"Whew, now *that* was some grub. These guys know how to throw a feast."

"You can say that again. Not only did they cook with sugar and pepper, they even brought up fruits from the south. Let's not forget about the massages the girls are getting either. Given this world's living standards, this is quite the hospitality they're showing us."

"Yeah, not to mention the extra somethin'-somethin' the two of us are getting after this. Heh-heh-heh."

"...Your tastes are as blatant as ever."

"Hey, what's wrong with a dude likin' the ladies? If anything, it's a sign I'm a healthy young adult. Man, thinking 'bout Sanya and Irina with boobs full o' bounce… The memory alone's got me going!"

A lecherous look spread across Masato's face as he thought back on the two rabbit-eared *byuma* dancers who'd entertained during dinner.

After Tsukasa and Masato had split up with the girls, they were quietly offered a slightly different sort of perk than the aromatherapy massages. Later that night, they could have any dancer they liked sent up to their chambers.

Not to chat, of course, and not to play Uno, either.

"So, Tsukasa, who'd you pick?"

"I'm not going to dignify that with a response."

"C'mon, man, just tell me. I swear I won't blab to the others, 'kay? Who's your type?"

"What is this, some sort of school camping trip?"

However, seeing that Masato was in unusually high spirits, Tsukasa let out an exasperated sigh and answered, "If you must know, I graciously declined the offer."

"What?! Why?"

"I wasn't interested."

"*What?* …You're not interested in chicks? You're freaking me out a little here, dude."

"Quit scooting away from me. And stop hiding your chest like that. It's unbecoming. What I mean is, I have no interest in a purely carnal experience."

"Wait, seriously?"

"Very."

A look of disbelief crossed Masato's face. Every single one of the *byuma* dancers had been an unparalleled hottie. It was beyond Masato's ability to even picture someone not being interested in such tempting bodies.

And yet...

"*Sigh*. Y'know, that's actually pretty like you."

"My sincerity?"

"How stupidly stubborn you are."

After thinking for a bit, Masato realized that it would've been far stranger if his blockhead of a friend had told him that he'd called some girl up to his room because she had a nice ass or something.

"I feel like that sorta old-fashioned thinking about gender relations is just gonna hurt you in life, but I guess it's not really my place to criticize."

"That's right. Everyone's entitled to their own views and values."

"I feel you, I feel you. Welp, if you say you're not interested, that's your business."

Tsukasa's refusal wasn't going to hurt Masato, of course.

"I guess that leaves tonight's special service to me, huh. Don't worry, though. I'll make sure to enjoy it enough for the both of us."

"Oh, that won't be necessary. I turned it down for you, too."

"You bastard, you did WHAAAAAAAAAAT?!"

Upon hearing the world-shattering news, Masato let out a furious roar and launched a kick at Tsukasa's side. Faced with such an attack, Tsukasa merely parried with his palm as he talked his friend down.

"All right, settle down there."

"Like hell I'm gonna settle down! What kind of a dick move was that?! You were literally just talking about personal freedom!"

"That's true, and if we were on Earth, I would be content with leaving you to your salacious ways. Right now, though, we're acting as this world's angels. If you were unfortunate enough to get someone pregnant, what do you think would happen?"

"Urk..."

Tsukasa's rational reasoning left Masato at a loss for words.

At the moment, they were attempting to establish the world's first democratic nation. However, if they went about that task as humans, then when they eventually left and returned to Earth, there was a danger that whoever took over their posts would simply create a new aristocracy. In order to avoid that, the Prodigies were masquerading as divine beings.

If any of them slept with someone from this world and accidentally got them pregnant, though, there was a chance that could lay the seeds for a new monarchy.

Masato knew that. He understood it from a rational perspective, but he didn't like the idea of accepting it. He was already in the mood. Getting blue-balled now meant he wasn't going to be able to sleep.

Dammit, guess I'm gonna have to sneak out of my room tonight to get me some...

"And just so you know, you won't be sneaking out tonight, either. I had them put us in the same room, you and I. And there's no escape from me."

"You monster...!"

"Don't worry. If it gets too bad, I'd be happy to wait outside the room while you attend to your needs."

"How fuckin' considerate of you! Shit! Not only do I have to cancel plans with a bunch of babes, now I gotta room with you, too?! God fuckin' dammit!!"

Abruptly thrust from the highest of highs to the lowest of lows, Masato plopped his elbows on the tub's rim and cradled his head in his hands.

Suddenly, a new voice entered the conversation.

"Tsukes, Massy, we're back! Sounds like you two're enjoying the water!"

Having finished their aromatherapy massages, the girls flooded into the bath area with Shinobu leading the charge.

They hadn't come to soak, of course.

All of them were adorned in white gowns and leaf tiaras, like Greek goddesses.

"Good, you're here," replied Tsukasa, not perturbed in the slightest. He adjusted his loincloth and greeted his teammates.

The plan had been to meet in the bath to discuss future strategies.

"Were the massages everything you ever dreamed of?" Tsukasa inquired. "I heard they use top-shelf balms normally reserved for the empress herself."

"Oh, it was the *best*! I've never been so happy to have been born a girl!" chirped Shinobu.

"My sentiments exactly," Keine agreed. "We also learned that the ointments were created using spirit magic. It would seem that this world's magic is used for more than just warfare."

"That's right," answered Tsukasa. "According to the First-Class Mage we captured back in Findolph, the academy's Second-Class Mages aren't experienced enough at controlling spirits to be trusted as combatants. Their jobs consist largely of industrial and cleaning work. The closest any of them get to a battlefield is when they clean equipment and strip rust off of armor."

"Ha-ha!" laughed Aoi. "Cleaning, of all things?"

"It lets them practice manipulating spirits, so it acts as part of their training. That First-Class Mage I mentioned, Gale, is actually having Lyrule do something similar."

"Come to think of it, Lyrule handled the laundry at our field hospital in Archride. I recall being impressed at how she cleaned everything so thoroughly without any bleach, but now it makes sense. She was using magic, I take it?" inquired Keine.

"According to Gale, she shies away from using magic that *hurts others*, but overall, her ability to control spirits exceeds that of even the Imperial Prime Baptists at the empire's mint. They're the mages who

©Sacraneco

use spirit magic to remove impurities from their gold and increase the quality of their currency."

The sway that an Imperial Prime Baptist held over spirits was considered exceptional, even among Imperial Prime Mages. They were responsible for maintaining the empire's standards for its coinage. Only the best of the best got to work there.

To everyone's surprise, Lyrule had outdone them only a month after her awakening. Evidently, her powers really were something special.

"…The mysteries about her just keep piling up, don't they?" Tsukasa said.

"Yup," Shinobu replied. "Oh, by the way, why's Massy look like the world just ended on him?"

"Don't mind him. It's not important."

"Ah. So the you-know-what?"

"It's important to *me*, all right?! Just because—"

But before Masato could begin his rant in earnest, he spotted something interesting out of the corner of his eye.

A moment later, all the despondency vanished from his face, replaced by an ill-natured grin.

"Hang on, who's that blond cutie over there? C'mon, introduce me to her already."

"I'll hit you, you know?!" Akatsuki, who was wearing the same getup as all the girls, took his leaf tiara and hurled it at Masato.

"Ha-ha-ha. Hey, it's not my fault you came back all cute and spruced up."

"It *is* your fault! This asshole here is one thing, but, Tsukasa, you can't just abandon me like that! Why didn't you stop the maids for me?!" There was no attempt on Akatsuki's part to hide his indignation.

Upon inspection, it appeared that the scarlet had yet to fully fade from the magician's cheeks. He must really have been embarrassed.

"I am sorry about that," Tsukasa apologized. "But Marquis Conrad was watching, so I couldn't say anything. If any of us had pointed out the servants' mishap, there was a chance they would've been executed for it."

"I mean...Shinobu explained that all to me, but you're *you*. Couldn't you have found some way to save me from the maids while still smoothing things over with that guy?"

"...Maybe, but like I told you before, you're still acting as the centerpiece of the Seven Luminaries faith, so it would be a big problem if anything happened to you. That's why I'm trying to have you stay near Aoi whenever possible. Even with the imperially appointed lord ousted, the domain still identifies as part of the Freyjagard Empire, so we're technically in hostile territory right now. Merchant and I are no slouches, but Aoi can do a far better job of defending you than even the both of us combined."

"Urgh..."

"It's fine, Prince. You got a sweet massage out of the deal, didn't you?" Masato needled with a grin.

"It's not fine! Think of how embarrassing it would've been if they'd realized I was a guy halfway through!"

"Huh? Wait, you mean they never noticed?"

"Uhh... Th-that's not..." Realizing he'd said too much, Akatsuki tried frantically to backpedal.

"Nope," Shinobu declared.

"They never even seemed suspicious, that they did not," added Aoi.

Without even the slightest hesitation, the girls completely blew poor Akatsuki's cover.

"That's...impressive," Tsukasa noted.

"Yeah, man, not just any guy could pull *that* off."

"Maaan... You two suck! Screw you guys!"

Akatsuki turned his back on his two earnestly impressed friends and began cradling his knees in his hands.

Admittedly, Tsukasa did feel embarrassed that his praise had set off Akatsuki's habitual coping mechanism. Right as he was about to apologize, Tsukasa suddenly had the feeling that he was being watched very intently.

Hmm?

The gaze was timid but intense all the same.

When Tsukasa turned to look, he discovered Ringo with her hands over her crimson face staring at him from between the gaps in her fingers.

"Hwa-wa-wa…"

She didn't seem to have realized he'd noticed her. Her fervent, watery eyes remained transfixed on his loincloth-covered body. Seeing Ringo like that reminded Tsukasa of the time right after they'd finished building the bathhouse in Elm. Back then, fraught as she was by her leaf swimsuit attire, she'd snatched glances at him in exactly the same way. Tsukasa didn't find it particularly odd, however.

He didn't agree with everything from Masato's last speech. Still, it was true that having interest in bodies of the opposite sex was merely a sign that one was a healthy young adult. That was why the Tsukasa merely glanced away, pretending not to have noticed anything.

A few moments later, the conversation began to shift from the topic of Akatsuki to the Blue Brigade.

"Be that as it may, we're getting quite the warm welcome here, that we are. When soldiers and civilians alike are impoverished from the battle against Gustav, is it truly all right that they pamper us in so grand a fashion?" Aoi asked.

"It's *because* they're hurting that they wanna avoid picking a fight with us Seven Luminaries," explained Masato. "They don't wanna make enemies out of us, especially not after we claimed two imperial domains in a single week. Hell, they're probably freaking out right now."

"Still, it would be optimal if things could be worked out diplomatically. Like it or not, more fighting inevitably leads to more dead and injured. What are your thoughts on the matter, Tsukasa? Can we make allies with the people of the Blue Brigade?" Upon hearing Keine's question, Tsukasa shot Shinobu a glance.

"Yeah, gimme a sec," she responded. Kneeling down, Shinobu pressed her ear against the wet floor. She was using sound to search the area around them. After a little while, she lifted her torso and gave him the thumbs-up.

"'Kay, we're good. The only others within two hundred feet are the pair replenishing the kindling in the boiler room. Neither of them is close enough to eavesdrop. Between that and the Blue Brigade's lack of mages, we don't have to worry about being overheard."

"Much obliged."

After Shinobu confirmed that there weren't any unwanted parties listening in, Tsukasa thanked her, then finally answered Keine's question.

"To sum it up…that won't be possible."

A few hours earlier, the High School Prodigies had come to Nord Villa's lounge as representatives of the Seven Luminaries to meet with Marquis Conrad, the scrawny old man serving as the Blue Brigade's leader.

"Well, well, well! I must thank you all for coming such a distance for this meeting. I am Rommel von Conrad. The Blue Brigade's former leader, Granzham von Blumheart, met an unfortunate end in battle, so I will be governing the Gustav domain in his place."

"I am Tsukasa Mikogami, entrusted with matters of government by God Akatsuki of the Seven Luminaries. We're grateful for this opportunity to speak with you."

After exchanging a handshake with Tsukasa, Conrad bowed in an overly excessive show of respect.

"Oh, not at all. Our victory over Gustav would hardly have been possible if not for the help of your fellow angel, Shinobu. No thanks we offered you could ever be sufficient. To think that you weren't a Yamato survivor but an angel from the heavens. If you had only said something sooner, we would never have given you such a dangerous role…"

Conrad's apology carried the unfortunate implication that they'd given Shinobu a dangerous task *because* they'd mistaken her for a Yamato survivor, but Tsukasa wasn't childish enough to let his displeasure show on his face.

"Well, now that we've acknowledged our mutual gratitude, perhaps it's time to get to the matter at hand," Tsukasa offered.

Conrad agreed obediently and showed the Seven Luminaries to their chairs.

Then, the meeting between the representatives of the Seven Luminaries and the Blue Brigade began in earnest.

"The matter at hand, naturally, is the relationship between your Blue Brigade and our Seven Luminaries."

"…You wish to know if we accept the terms of your People's Revolution, which seeks equality for all, is that right?"

Tsukasa replied with a nod.

"The teachings of the Seven Luminaries would see inequality stamped out. Suppose the Blue Brigade is amenable to such ideals. In that case, we see no reason to take military action as we did against Archride and Buchwald. On the contrary, we would welcome your cooperation in enacting our reforms. That would, of course, include standing against the empire, which no doubt opposes our teachings."

"The Blue Brigade began as a group of nobles seeking to help the suffering commoners. So naturally, we applaud your concern toward reform. However..." Conrad let his words trail off somewhat ominously.

"Is there some problem?" Tsukasa asked.

"...I'm afraid so. A great number of people are wary of founding a nation without a noble ruling class. It's a simple fact that not every member of the Blue Brigade is on the same page."

"In other words, you're concerned that the masses' low levels of education will give rise to unstable governance?"

"...Y-yes. Personally, even I have my doubts that...the common people can handle the burden of law... Such things are difficult to judge, so I'm afraid I cannot give you an answer at present."

"Do you mean to say that you won't cooperate with us?"

Conrad shook his head so frantically his neck seemed liable to break.

"O-oh, heavens no! I'm not saying anything of the sort! The Blue Brigade is in full favor of equality for all! We have every desire to cooperate with you in the fullest, I swear! ...*Making* that choice requires greater conviction, however. After all, this is no feudal lord we'd be going to war with; this is the emperor himself. And we're not even fully certain your ways would be for the good of the people yet. We of the Blue Brigade have a duty to the populace of the Gustav domain to deliberate carefully—"

"—For the sake of their future," Conrad added after a moment. "So...might I request...we have some more time to see how the situation will evolve?"

The old man wanted to defer his decision.

"Hmm..."

Tsukasa went quiet for a bit, then nodded in the affirmative. "...Very well. We of the Seven Luminaries respect how uneasy you feel at the prospect of abolishing the noble ruling class you're so accustomed to. It's like crossing a suspension bridge over a valley with fog so thick you can't see an inch in front of your face. How can you tell that the bridge is sturdy? As a leader of others, your desire to do your due diligence is commendable."

In any given village, the number of fully literate people was often low enough to count on one hand. Conrad's concerns were perfectly legitimate. If his domain democratized thoughtlessly, there was a good chance it would throw the government into chaos. None of the world's countries, least of all the Freyjagard Empire, would fail to capitalize on that opportunity. Tsukasa was well aware of that, which was why he was trying to garner the nobles' support.

Pressing for a hasty answer was an unwise tactic, but Tsukasa did not relent merely after demonstrating that he understood Conrad's position.

"At the same time, however, I believe your fears can be quelled by observing the state of the Findolph, Archride, and Buchwald domains. So take that time and use it to remove whatever doubts you have." Tsukasa's tone was amicable, but he was unmistakably laying on the pressure.

"Th-thank you for your c-consideration in this matter…!" Conrad praised with a stiff smile. Being allowed to defer his decision was probably as much as he'd hoped for.

As for the High School Prodigies, that was a point they'd decided to cede beforehand. In short, the first topic on the agenda had resolved in largely the way both parties had expected.

However—

"…Regretfully, there's one issue that cannot wait."

—with the opening bits of business out of the way, Tsukasa moved right on to the day's second, and most important, topic.

"Wh-what might that be?"

"It should go without saying that we must restore living standards for the Gustav domain's citizens."

Tsukasa had heard stories from Shinobu, and he'd seen the domain's state of affairs on their journey to Nord Villa. Those alone had been more than enough to let him know just how dire things were. The people's quality of life had deteriorated to the point where they couldn't recover on their own, and Tsukasa believed it essential that the local governing body intervene as quickly as possible.

To that end...

"I understand that Duke Gustav imposed ludicrously high taxes in order to fund a gold statue of Emperor Lindworm. It seems to me that the reasonable course of action would be to break it down for gold bullion, sell it on the marketplace, and use that money to buy food and provisions from other domains. To facilitate this, the Order of the Seven Luminaries is prepared to dispatch our angel entrusted by God Akatsuki with matters of commerce. How does that sound? We wouldn't expect any compensation for the service, naturally."

Tsukasa was offering the unconditional aid of the Seven Luminaries. There shouldn't have been any reason for the Blue Brigade to turn them down.

"...W-well, you see, about that." Conrad's gaze darted from corner to corner. When he eventually found his words again, his voice was pained. "I'm afraid there's a bit of a problem. It would appear that, before we made our move in Millevana, the gold statue in question was sent to Drachen, the imperial capital, and we haven't been able to locate it."

"That's quite concerning. How do you propose to offer economic relief to the people, then?"

After hearing Conrad's confession, Tsukasa narrowed his gaze on him probingly and asked for his backup plan. The older man's brow furrowed in discomfort. Soon enough, however, Conrad opened his eyes wide with renewed determination.

"To be perfectly honest…helping the populace recover simply isn't possible without the funds from that statue! We of the Blue Brigade lack the power to rescue the people in their time of need. So though it is shameful of me to beg, could I ask that the Seven Luminaries' God Akatsuki use his power to save the people from starvation?!" As he wrung the voice out of his throat to make his desperate plea to the High School Prodigies, Conrad bowed low enough that his forehead was touching the table.

A noble, bowing to people young enough to be his grandchildren for the sake of the common folk was an act of overflowing courtliness. Given that Conrad was beating around the bush when it came to enacting reforms, yet asking loud and clear when he needed help, it came off as profoundly brazen, however.

The Gustav domain was the dukedom entrusted with managing all four northern domains. It was nearly twice as large as the Archride domain, the next largest of the four in terms of territory. More land meant more population. Having to prop up the massive Gustav domain's economy would place an immense burden on its three remote neighbors. It wasn't a task that even the Prodigies could've agreed to easily.

"I understand. The Order of the Seven Luminaries offers you its full cooperation." Despite any such difficulties, Tsukasa accepted without so much as hesitating.

"Tr-truly?!" Conrad had never imagined that he'd secure the assistance of the Seven Luminaries so effortlessly. With a shocked expression, he double-checked to make sure he'd heard correctly.

Tsukasa's second answer was the same as his first.

"Yes. We descended from the heavens to save people from their suffering. It would make no sense for us to abandon them now. We'll start by providing food and medicine from Findolph, Archride, and Buchwald to supplant Gustav's shortages. That should help to build up the health of the populace." For the first time in the discussion, Tsukasa offered the other man a smile.

"Given the size of the Gustav domain, however, surpluses from the three other domains may prove insufficient. We'll need to go through Gustav to conduct trade with the empire's eastern and western regions, as well as its capital, to secure stores of food. However, that will necessitate that we have free travel across Gustav's borders to conduct business. There's no other way about it. Is that acceptable?"

"Y-yes! Of course! I have no reason to refuse that request! You fine people can come and go as you please without tariffs, and the trade routes and ports are yours to use freely!"

"I appreciate your generosity."

"N-nonsense! It is I who should be thanking you! The people of the Gustav domain will live to see another year thanks to you!" His voice trembling with joy, Conrad gave Tsukasa another desk-scraping bow.

As Tsukasa looked down at Conrad's head, though, the smile quickly faded from his face.

"Allying ourselves won't be possible? The gentleman seemed interested in cooperation, did he not?" As Aoi thought back to their meeting with the Blue Brigade, she asked Tsukasa to explain his reasoning.

"I don't suspect they bear any animosity toward the Seven Luminaries. And when he said he wanted to cooperate with us, I believe he was telling the truth. I wouldn't be at all shocked to learn he told the empire the same thing, however. After all, if they'd completely cut ties with the empire, there would be no reason for them not to work side by side with us."

Keine concurred. "Quite so. In fact, they would want to join forces with us as quickly as possible to be ready if the empire decided to take action."

"Exactly. Right now, the Blue Brigade is wavering. They're trying to figure out who to support—the Seven Luminaries or the Freyjagard Empire."

Tsukasa's assessment of the situation was right on the mark.

A few days before Conrad's meeting with the Seven Luminaries, he'd sent a message to Neuro ul Levias, one of the Four Imperial Grandmasters standing in for Emperor Lindworm. The ruler of the Freyjagard Empire was off on his expedition to the New World. *"We of the Blue Brigade slew the villain who was willfully weakening the empire from within, but we bear no hostility toward the Freyjagard Empire as a whole. Long live the law of survival of the fittest."* It had contained the exact same sentiment he'd gone on to express to the Seven Luminaries earlier that day. Simply put, Conrad was fence-sitting.

"Hey, I mean, given the Blue Brigade's position, you can't blame him for playing the opportunist. No matter who he picks, it's gonna mean war, so obviously, he wants to play both sides for a bit to give his exhausted army time to recover. What other choice does he have, being sandwiched between two major powers like that?" Masato inquired.

Tsukasa nodded in agreement. "Merchant has it right. It's hard to consider that an act of bad faith. No, the reason I said we won't be able to ally ourselves with the Blue Brigade is a wholly separate matter… The thing is, Sir Conrad told us an unforgivable lie."

"He…lied?"

"That's right. He told us that he didn't know where the gold statue was. The moment he said so, however, the movement of his eyes, the shifting of his tongue, and the creases in his face all signaled that it was a complete and utter falsehood. He knows *exactly* where the statue is. I'd bet he's already gotten ahold of it."

"Wh—?! Is that true?!"

"I don't have any hard evidence, but…I've never failed to detect a liar when talking face-to-face."

Tsukasa himself was certain of Conrad's deception, as was another member of the Prodigies.

"Yeah, I figured. Honestly, I was thinkin' the same thing," Shinobu agreed.

"What tipped you off?" Tsukasa questioned.

"Duke Gustav had this aide named Oscar, and he was a spy for the Blue Brigade. Oscar was the one in charge of shipping off the gold statue, so if he knew how soon the coup was, why actually send the statue to the capital? So, y'know, I figured something was up."

"Yeah, that's definitely weird… Actually, it's sus as hell," Masato observed.

"So wait, that old guy Conrad's trying to steal the gold statue for himself?" Akatsuki asked, rejoining the conversation. Masato gave the inquiry a nod.

"Makes you wonder about their former leader, Count…uh, Blumheart, right? The Blue Brigade nobles could've orchestrated that 'battle-field death' of his."

"Yeah, I figure that's pretty likely," Shinobu agreed.

"Either way, no group that's willing to steal a gold statue for personal gain while they have commoners eating one another just to survive will ever actually get behind our 'equality for all' reforms. Before long, they'll try to mend relations with the empire and turn on us," Tsukasa stated flatly.

Such a deduction on the prodigal politician's part only raised more questions from the others.

"But if you knew all that, why'd you tell them that we'd pay for the restoration efforts?" Shinobu pressed.

One certainly had to wonder why Tsukasa offered such assistance.

"Couldn't we just have Shinobu go track down the statue? That way, we wouldn't have to spend any of our own money, and we'd be able to expose those Blue Brigade geezers for what they are," suggested Akatsuki.

"Indeed. That would be preferable, would it not?" Aoi added.

"Yeah, it'd only take me three days to hunt it down. What's our angle?"

Tsukasa shook his head, however, and refused Akatsuki, Aoi, and Shinobu's suggestion.

"That won't be necessary."

"Why not? Is three days too slow?" Shinobu asked.

Again, Tsukasa shook his head. "There are two reasons. The first…is that we still haven't confirmed Gustav's death. As I understand it, the man was downright obsessed with the statue. If he is still alive, stealing it back will be his top priority. And that's all the more reason not to have it anywhere near us."

"Ah, you're right…" Shinobu had experienced Gustav's power firsthand, so she knew all too well the danger the man posed.

To put it in terms of modern firepower, he was like a soldier equipped with a flamethrower and a grenade launcher. Having someone like that employing guerilla tactics against them was not a position the Prodigies wanted to be in.

Shinobu and Aoi could hold their own, of course, but Gustav would torch any other member of the group without much trouble. Such a scenario was exactly what Tsukasa was trying to avoid.

"So we're basically using the Blue Brigade as our shields?" Akatsuki asked.

"That's part of it, but there's a more important reason."

Tsukasa paused for a moment, then explained.

"Even if we found that statue and exposed the Blue Brigade's corruption, it wouldn't actually end up hurting their cause."

"Why not?" Shinobu wondered aloud.

"'Cause of how loyal the Gustav domain's people are to the Blue Brigade now...right?"

"Merchant's got it," Tsukasa affirmed.

As far as the masses were concerned, the Blue Brigade were the heroes who saved them from the wicked Gustav. In their eyes, that group could do no wrong.

"Even if we were to find the statue and expose the greedy nobles for their wrongdoing, they could just claim that Gustav's secretary acted alone. The public would have no reason not to believe them. In fact, even if people didn't buy that kind of excuse, they wouldn't care. For them, anything is preferable to Gustav," explained Tsukasa.

"Ah...," muttered Akatsuki.

"At that point, all Sir Conrad has to do is return the statue, and they'll forever hail him as the 'model knight who righted his subordinates' misdeed.' Then, our position will weaken for having accused him. If that happened, we'd be done for. Nothing we did from then on would ever earn back the trust of the citizens.

"The Blue Brigade has the confidence of the Gustav domain. Even if they're wholly in the wrong, any aggressive action we take against them carries considerable political risk. Human beings like to assume that anyone they believe in is always right. Whatever plan we choose needs to take that psychological habit into account. For now, we need to win the people over gradually."

"An astute observation. So that's why you agreed to handle the restoration efforts," Keine deduced.

"Yes. The more resources we put in, the less responsibility the Blue Brigade will take on. These are the nobles who stole the gold statue for personal gain, after all. If they can get someone else to pay for the recovery, nothing would make them happier."

"So *while overlooking their corruption*, you plan to have us Seven

Luminaries carry out as much of the restoration efforts ourselves as possible and win the people over that way?" reasoned Masato.

"Exactly," Tsukasa replied. "Right now, the Gustav commoners' trust lies *solely* in their saviors: the Blue Brigade. If we bring their misdeeds to light, they won't be happy, but they'll continue looking to the aristocracy for leadership. They've little other option, after all.

"It'll be a different story once our group grows more popular and we establish ourselves as a realistic alternative by facilitating the domain's rehabilitation. That will be the moment to expose the Blue Brigade for what it really is. In the meantime, the gold statue will serve perfectly to distract Sir Conrad and his allies from our proselytizing. They can line their pockets all they want. Unlike hearts and minds, money can easily be recovered by force."

With that, Tsukasa swept his gaze out over his assembled friends.

"It's for those reasons that we won't be attacking the Blue Brigade for the time being. I hope that's enough to convince you all."

"""_____"""

All six of the other High School Prodigies nodded.

"Good. On that note, let's go over your individual assignments."

Having received their approval, Tsukasa began to distribute the new orders.

"Now, most of them haven't changed much from our time in Findolph. Akatsuki, I'd like you to travel around and use your magic shows to win the people over. Aoi, you go with him and serve as his assistant and bodyguard."

"Understood."

"Maaan… Another grueling itinerary for me, huh?"

"Keine, your job is to take charge of improving health conditions for the impoverished. We're in a bitter race against time on that front, so your work is going to be the most labor-intensive, but I'm counting on you nonetheless."

"Very well, then. A doctor who balks in the face of adversity is no doctor at all, I daresay. Still, the Gustav domain is quite large. I'll need plenty of qualified hands to help."

"We'll get you as many knights and farmers as those sectors can spare. The domain is also home to a healer's association, so we'll arrange for their cooperation, too. Luckily, it's winter right now. With no farm work to do, securing human resources should be relatively easy."

"That would be a big help. Fortunately, malnourishment itself can be treated remotely. So long as I have sufficient laborers, food, and medical supplies to assemble treatment packages, I should have the region in good health in no time."

"I'm glad to hear it. As far as securing and distributing the food and medical supplies in question goes… Merchant, that's where you come in."

"With Gustav's ports, getting the stuff'll be a cinch. Distributing it's gonna be trickier, though. Gathering up food and supplies from Archride and Buchwald and spreading it throughout Gustav is gonna take more carriages than we've got."

Most of the horses in the Gustav domain had been killed and eaten already.

However…

"Back when Shinobu first told me about the state of affairs here in Gustav, I had Bearabbit deal with that particular problem in advance." Tsukasa turned to Ringo. "How are those freight trucks I requested coming along?"

The scientist tottered over and quietly whispered in Tsukasa's ear, her eyes averted from the young man's bare torso all the while.

"Um…from the text Bearabbit sent me…everyone in the Man-ufacturing District is working hard…and they have twenty ten-ton off-road trucks…ready to go. They blasted a tunnel through the mountains…and the trucks are on their way here."

"What about the drivers?" Tsukasa asked.

"They're being run by copies of Bearabbit...so we're all good there."

"I appreciate the update." Tsukasa turned back and relayed Ringo's information to Masato. "...And there you have it."

"For real?! Damn, Ringo, you're like our very own Doraemon!"

"..."

Ringo didn't deal well with loud noises or voices, so her shoulders twitched at Masato's exclamation, but she quickly gave him a small V-for-victory sign with her hand.

Previously, Ringo hadn't been able to communicate with anyone other than Tsukasa, but after living together with the others in this new world, she was slowly adapting to interacting with them.

Masato responded to Ringo's nonverbal reply with a pleased grin.

"If we've got wheels, I'm all good. Consider the goods signed for, sealed, and delivered."

Tsukasa thanked Masato, then moved on to Shinobu.

"Now, Shinobu, you'll continue working alongside the Blue Brigade."

"You want me to keep an eye out and see if they're actin' fishy, right?"

"That's certainly part of it, but...I've heard that the Blue Brigade isn't necessarily monolithic. I want you to contact anyone you think is truly willing to cooperate with the Seven Luminaries. We'll need them, for when we found our nation."

"Recon and sowin' dissent, all at the same time? Well, I'll make it work," Shinobu said with a shrug.

"I know it's a difficult task, but given your abilities, I know you're up to it," Tsukasa encouraged.

"Sha-sha. Leave it to me."

Tsukasa then turned to the last member of the group, Ringo Oohoshi.

"Finally, Ringo. If our nation is to rise, there's something I need you to—"

As the white-haired young man tried to finish, however—

"Ah, hold on just a moment. I'm afraid that won't do."

—Keine interrupted and cut him off.

"Keine?"

"…?"

Tsukasa and Ringo cocked their heads to the side, and Keine elaborated.

"Ringo and Tsukasa, both of you are to take the next three days to recuperate. Doctor's orders."

"What on earth is this about?" Tsukasa insisted.

"If the two of you keep pushing yourselves like this, you're going to collapse. The scent of your perspiration, your glossy sebaceous glands, the state of your nails and mucous membranes… Observation of these external factors allows me to assess your health with as much accuracy as a blood test.

"The results of the visual analysis tell me that you both have severely compromised immune systems. If you continue at your current pace, Ringo will contract acute tonsillitis in five days, and Tsukasa will come down with bronchitis in a week's time. From there, it will take you both ten days to recover.

"That's a painful amount of time to lose, no? As for me, I'll have my hands full treating the commoners and soldiers injured in the previous battle, so I really can't have you two getting sick right now. Before that happens, I need you to rest and let your immune systems recover."

Hesitating for a moment, Tsukasa pictured just how badly a three-day break would set him back. "…Understood," he agreed after a short silence. "It pains me to take such a long vacation, but I'm not about to go against the professional opinion of Keine Kanzaki, prodigy doctor."

"I do so love an obedient patient," Keine cooed sweetly.

"To be frank, I did realize I was pushing myself and letting Ringo force herself as well..." Tsukasa let out a wry laugh, then addressed the group once more.

"Well, there you have it. I'm sorry to do this while you're all working so hard, but Ringo and I will be resting for the next few days."

"Y'know, I figured it'd happen to us all eventually, but I guess you two *really* don't know how to quit, do ya?" Masato remarked.

"Taking time to recuperate is important, that it is," added Aoi.

None of the others voiced any complaints about Keine's medical advice. They all knew that between Tsukasa's battles against the subjugating army and Ringo's manufacturing of the trucks and night-vision goggles, the two of them had been working nonstop for some time.

Thankful to have such understanding friends, Tsukasa replied, "Fair enough. Then recuperate, I shall."

Turning back to Ringo, Tsukasa offered her a suggestion.

"You know, Ringo, we don't get much time off like this. Spending it sleeping in our rooms would be dull, and I did have that thing I wanted to talk to you about. What do you say we spend the third day hanging out together in the city?"

"...?" Ringo immediately tilted her head to the side a bit. What she'd just heard had been so unexpected that her brain wasn't able to process it.

"Oh, a date? What a lovely idea," Keine said with a smile.

"Man, lucky... I wanna get a day off with Tsukasa," grumbled a certain short, blond boy.

"Akatsuki, m'lord, did we not spend that break together in Elm?" Aoi reminded.

"How was I supposed to rest when I had to spend the whole time with a girl? You even followed me into the bath! If anything, I was *more* tired afterward!"

"Show our girl a good time, Tsukasa," Shinobu remarked with a mischievous expression.

After hearing her friends' opinions on Tsukasa's proposal, Ringo finally understood what he'd suggested. Forgetting that she was around others—

"HUUUUUUUUUUUUUUUUUUH?!?!"

—Ringo let out a cry of disbelief at the top of her lungs.

CHAPTER 2

❧ Love-Huntress Ringo ❧

After their meeting with the Blue Brigade, Ringo went back to Dormundt and headed straight for her lab in the Manufacturing District.

"Bearabbit, Bearabbit, Bearabbiiiiit!"

"T-tail me what's wrong!"

"What do I do...? It's all so sudden, I just—I don't...!"

"Wh-what's going on? J-just calm down and tail me."

"I—I can't just calm down; it's not that easy..."

"Okay, then don't calm down, but either way, tail me what's going on!"

Not placating herself in the slightest, Ringo gesticulated wildly as she explained how Tsukasa had invited her on a date at the end of their three-day break.

Upon hearing that, the stumpy pink character on Bearabbit's display leaped up in surprise.

"A—a date with Tsukasa, you say?!"

"Hwah! Th-that's not what I said... We're just spending our day off together, that's all..."

"A bear-bones outing with just the two of you? I hate to be the bearer of good news, but that's a date! And a big chance fur you to deepen your bond with him! Looks like it's your lucky day!"

Bearabbit knew just how long Ringo had been harboring feelings for Tsukasa, so hearing about this sudden development was a thrill for him.

Ringo, on the other hand, glanced around timidly.

"B-b-but...I-I've never been on a date... I have no idea...where to go or what to wear... Wh-what if the conversation dies down when we're alone...a-and he starts thinking I'm boring...? Oh..."

The poor girl had never expected such a windfall of good fortune and hadn't been able to sort out her emotions yet. She was certainly happy about the date. Being able to spend time alone with Tsukasa was like a dream come true for Ringo.

Unfortunately, Ringo quickly began to doubt herself, and her mind filled with negative hypotheticals. Bearabbit, however, spoke to the troubled genius with confidence in his electronic voice.

"Heh-heh-heh... Ringo, just who exactly do you think I am?"

"?"

"I'm the all-purpose support robot designed to help you live your life, remember?! I always knew this day might come, so I aggregated all the hottest trends and put together a pawsome date plan and shopping list fur you!"

"R-really?!"

To Ringo, Bearabbit's words were a veritable ray of hope that shone down through dark clouds. Rushing over to the AI, Ringo pressed him for details.

"P-please, tell me—"

"Not so fast, now. I'm not just going to tail you for free. Putting it together took a lot of tailent, you know."

"Y-you're demanding payment from your creator?"

"Ringo, Ringo, Ringo. Don't look at it that way. Think of all the ways I've supported you, both in public and in private. Shouldn't you be showing me a little more gratitude? Maybe reflect on how rudely *you've been treating me. From now on, I don't want that cheap oil any-more. I want you to give me the good, dark stuff from the bottom of the can, like what Dorami got. If you can pawmise me that, I'll send you the data."*

"Hmph…"

Bearabbit put an image up on his display of him sticking his hand into a pot full of honey-colored oil, licking it, and spitting it out in disgust.

Ringo had no idea how her creation had grown so impudent. She even slightly regretted her decision to grant the AI such freedom and the ability to grow. Still, that data Bearabbit had was her only hope. Knowing that sometimes sacrifices had to be made for the greater good, Ringo acquiesced.

"F-fine. I promise, so tell me."

"Hooray! All right, I'm sending the data over."

Bearabbit's screen-displayed avatar threw its arms up in joy as he transmitted the special feature he'd assembled for Ringo's first date to her smartphone.

Its contents were split into three main sections:

"Top 100 Outfits to Wear When You Have No Confidence in Your Figure!"

"How to Lock Down a Smooch from the Guy of Your Dreams! This Winter's Newest Lip Balms!"

"A First Date Plan Even a Monkey Could Get Right! Tokyo Metropolis Area Edition."

Hurriedly, Ringo scanned over each article.

"Wow, it's all so detailed! It has lists of restaurants for lunch and dinner, lists of what to wear, even lists of what lip balm to use."

"I am equipped with the world's greatest supercomputer, you know. Putting it together was pawsitively a breeze!"

"This is amazing…"

Not only was the data thorough, it was laid out in an easy-to-understand manner. One shouldn't have expected less from an AI built by prodigy inventor Ringo Oohoshi. The sections on clothes and cosmetics even had 3D graphics. Bearabbit had really thought of everything. With this guide, Ringo had all she needed; it was perfect. Well, except for one small thing.

"By the way, Bearabbit…"

"What can I do you fur?"

"How am I supposed to buy any of this?"

"Tee-hee-hee. You've been hibernating up in space too long, haven't you? Down here on Earth, we've got an e-commerce site called Amazo-ness where you can get your paws on just about any… Oh."

That small thing was that on this world, Bearabbit's notes were useless.

"You're getting used tempura oil from now on."

"Expanda'd cooking oil?!?!"

Ringo's voice was ice-cold as she deleted the eighteen-gigabyte file from her phone.

"Ringo, Ringo, let's just paws and think about this. It's certainly pawsible that I went a little too far just now. Have I ever mentioned how grateful I am to you for creating me? From now on, I pawmise not to complain about getting the light, cruddy stuff from the top of the can, s-so please…anything but used tempura oil…"

"I was kidding."

It was true that she was a little miffed, but Ringo still knew that Bearabbit had put all that data together for her sake. She wasn't actually planning on giving him waste oil. Unfortunately, the fact remained that her last ray of hope had failed her.

Ringo heaved a deep sigh, then let out a defeated murmur. Considering the possibility that she was just going to fail and embarrass herself, she muttered, "…Maybe it would be better if I just tell him I can't go…"

"*You can't!*"

Bearabbit indignantly shot that idea down.

"*Chances like this bearly ever come around! If you don't bear your fangs now and strike, when will you?*"

"But, Bearabbit… I'll just mess it up…"

"*Are you going to let Lyrule snatch Tsukasa away fur herself?*"

"—!" Ringo recalled the scene from that fateful night. The image of Tsukasa's head resting gently on Lyrule's lap had been burned into the young woman's brain.

She hated it.

The moment Ringo saw it, pain shot through her heart as if a knife had stabbed her. With a shake of her head, she dispelled the vivid recollection.

"…I…don't want that."

Ringo had loved Tsukasa for so, so long. She didn't want to just give up without even telling him how she felt.

"*Then even if you're scared that you'll mess it up, you have to just go fur it. Luckily, you've got some beary lovely lady friends to help you out. You should go get them to teach you how to get close with guys!*"

"_____"

"*There's no claws for alarm—this is your big chance! Be sure not to waste it!*"

Bearabbit's words of encouragement finally convinced her.

He was right. Ringo had been carrying that unrequited love for so long. Now that her big break had arrived, she needed to act on it.

Ringo resolved to ask her friends how best to get close to boys. Unfortunately, if everyday conversations were like walls to her, then trying to ask for that kind of advice was like breaking through solid iron. When faced with the alternative of letting her moment slip through her fingers, though, Ringo didn't hesitate.

"You're...right. I'll...do my best!"

With lips pursed tight, Ringo summoned up all the courage her little heart could muster and made up her mind to go ask the other three female High School Prodigies how to flirt with a guy.

"A method to get close to a gentleman, you say?"

Ringo's first stop was with prodigy swordmaster Aoi Ichijou. Despite her face being flushed red in embarrassment, Ringo asked the question herself without relying on Bearabbit. Aoi didn't make fun of her in the slightest. She merely lent her an ear, then puffed her chest out with pride.

"Heh. I have experience accompanying many men, so naturally, I know a thing or two, that I do."

"M-many men?! Whoa!!" Ringo pressed on, her face growing ever redder. "D-does that mean...you've also...k-k-kissed a lot of them?"

"Kissed...locked lips, you mean? But of course. I've locked lips with gentlemen on numerous occasions, that I have. And from what they say, a kiss from me is top-notch."

"!!!"

The way Aoi licked her lips after her proud proclamation sent a soft shiver down Ringo's spine. The gesture, along with the confidence brimming from her expression, told Ringo that Aoi was 100 percent serious.

Wow... S-so mature..., Ringo thought, realizing that pretty girls really were in a league of their own. Even though they were the same age, Aoi clearly possessed far more experience with men than a shrimp like her. It was clear she'd come to the right person.

"Although even I can only boast a resuscitation rate of about 70 percent. Some wounds are simply too large, that they are."

"...Eh?"

"Facing down death together truly is the best way to grow close. Between the enemies you slay and the comrades you lose, the bonds you form as survivors are as hard as steel. You become as close as family, even."

That was when Ringo finally realized that what she'd asked and what Aoi was talking about were two wholly different things.

"N-not that kind of bond... I, um, I'm talking about r-romantic bonds..."

"Hmm? Facing down death together causes love to bloom all the time, albeit largely between men."

"...?!" Ringo felt as though she had just been made privy to an incredible piece of information, but that wasn't what she was after, either.

"I-is there no way to get close...without...death involved?" Ringo made an attempt to get the conversation back on track.

"That proves trickier, that it does. Men have a way of looking down on us women. It's critical that you take him down first, to prove that you're stronger. To that end, I recommend aiming squarely for the crotch...the 'family jewels,' so to speak. Doing so should prove singularly effective.

"Ringo, m'lady, your stature will make kicking tricky, so I suggest grabbing hold of them and squeezing tight.

"That will render any man powerless, no matter how brawny they may be. That is simply how men are built, that it is."

Unfortunately, it didn't seem like Aoi had the answers that Ringo was looking for. Maybe she had been the wrong person to ask. Aoi was pretty and had many male friends, but she didn't seem interested in romance whatsoever.

"Th-thanks... I'll be sure...to keep that in mind..."

"Godspeed, m'lady. Remember to aim for his weak spot, and you'll be set, that you will!"

"A way to deepen your bond with a man?"

Next, Ringo turned to prodigy doctor Keine Kanzaki. Keine thought for a moment, then turned the question back on Ringo.

"Hmm. As a friend or as a lover? The methodology varies considerably between the two."

That was certainly true. Ringo had to admit that if she'd been clearer on that point, Aoi may have provided more useful information.

Ringo fought through her bashfulness and answered, "L-lo... lover...I guess."

"Hmm-hmm. Right, right. I see how it is." Keine seemed to have sensed something from Ringo's reply, but she avoided elaborating on what it was. "First, it's key that you find yourself alone with him. Taking a mutual day off and going on a date is ideal.

"Enjoy the sights, eat something tasty, and gradually close the distance between the two of you. Even if you get embarrassed, you absolutely mustn't look away from him. When a woman looks at someone she likes, her pupils dilate. Those larger pupils are a physiological mechanism your body uses to make you look cuter. It's important that you make full use of that and show off your adorable self."

W-wow... Ringo's eyes opened wide in surprise. She hadn't known about that trick.

Keine had a different view on things, and Ringo was overjoyed to get advice from her. She needed to make sure she didn't miss a thing. With an earnest expression on her face, Ringo jotted everything Keine was saying down on her notepad.

"Once you've grown familiar, that's where the chloroform comes in."

"Chloro…chlorowhat?!"

"Chloroform, I said. You'll want to soak a handkerchief in it and use it to knock him out."

"?!?!"

"From there, you drag him to a secluded spot and strip off his pants and undergarments."

"?!?!?!"

"Afterward, do just as you were taught in sex ed class. Take the ◆◆◆◆◆ of the man you're interested in, △△△△△△ it into your ○○○○○○, and ✕✕✕✕✕✕✕✕✕. If his ◆◆◆◆◆ doesn't react, △△△△△△ prostaglandin E1 directly into the erectile tissue. That should give you a good three hours to ✕✕✕✕✕✕✕✕✕.

"Now, I myself don't have any experience dealing with men romantically, but speaking as a doctor, I can assure you that's the most efficient way for two people to deepen their relationship. I hope you found that helpful."

"Gulp…"

As Keine finished her explanation, Ringo's eyes were spinning so fast she had to sit herself down. The insane logic that all Ringo had to do was make a baby was far too radical for her to handle.

Ringo did have to admit that Tsukasa would likely accept any child of his, no matter how it was conceived, but—

Th-there's no way I can do something like that!

—she had no intention of putting Keine's suggestion into practice.

That was not to suggest that Ringo hadn't found the lecture helpful in some way.

"…F-for the future, maybe" was the best she could manage in reply.

"I'm glad to hear it. Best of luck in your endeavor, Ringo."

"Wh-what should I do...?"

Having returned to her room, Ringo cradled her head in her hands. Much to her surprise, the two people she'd been counting on had been no help at all.

"They're both so pretty, but they both bearly had any experience with guys, huh."

"Yeah..."

When Ringo thought about it, though, she realized how self-reliant Aoi and Keine were. Both of them spent all their time on battlefields, honing their skills and living as they liked. Neither of them had time for something like love.

The same could've been said of all the High School Prodigies.

Ringo's last hope was prodigy journalist Shinobu Sarutobi. She was no different, however. Ever since middle school, she'd spent all her time flitting about political and business circles and their under-bellies, wielding her powers as a preeminent reporter as she saw fit.

Despite the ninja's good looks, there was a good chance she sported no romantic experience, either.

Ringo was worried, but she didn't have anywhere else to turn. She followed through with her plan and called Shinobu, who'd stayed behind in the Gustav domain.

Immediately, Shinobu answered the phone.

"H'lo?"

"H-hello... It's Ringo..."

"Ringo? Well, there's a surprise. It's not every day I get a call from you. Whassup?"

"I, um...I had something...I wanted to ask your advice about..."

"Who, li'l ol' me? Well, don't keep a girl hanging, now."

A little concerned that Shinobu's conversational tempo would end up sweeping her away, Ringo explained the situation.

"I—I was wondering if, um…you could teach me…how to get close…to a g-guy…"

Shinobu, ever quick on the uptake, immediately realized what she was talking about.

"Aha. Given the timing, I'm guessin' this is about Tsukes, riiiiight?"

"!!!"

All at once, Ringo's face turned a crimson shade at having been so handily exposed. Steeling herself, she responded in the affirmative.

"…Y-yes."

"Lyrule's really got you worried, huh?"

Shinobu was reading Ringo like a book. Such perceptivity was admittedly frightening to Ringo.

"Y-yeah…" With little other recourse, she confirmed Shinobu's guess, however. It was taking every bit of courage that Ringo had just to take advantage of her once-in-a-lifetime opportunity. This was no time to hold back or play dumb.

"Hee-hee. Glad you're bein' honest! Let me tell you, Ringo, you came to the right gal! After all, I'm a kunoichi—*a literal pro when it comes to honeypots! Trappin' the fellas so they can't get away is my specialty!"*

Ringo frantically corrected her. "B-but I don't want to trap him… I just want to get closer…normally."

Already, Ringo felt like she was about to get more advice in the same vein as Keine's. Shinobu was quick to discard Ringo's concerns, however.

"So green! You're greener than a Granny Smith apple, Ringo! Love is a hunt! Traps or not, you gotta catch your prey somehow! Lyrule might look timid, but she comes on real strong!"

"Sh-she does?!"

"From what I hear, though my info's secondhand from Massy. Remember how when everyone was gonna go save Lyrule and Tsukes

opposed it? Afterward, he was avoiding her and beatin' himself up pretty bad about it. He didn't think he was worthy of her thanks."

"Really…?" Ringo hadn't heard anything about that. But if that was the case, then why had Tsukasa been resting so intimately on her lap?

As if sensing that unspoken inquiry, Shinobu answered it immediately.

"When Lyrule heard how Tsukes was beating himself up, she barged right into the room he'd been cooping himself up in and forced him to acknowledge her gratitude.

"I'm tellin' you, Lyrule isn't some demure little princess. And plucky girls like her are real popular with the fellas. At the end of the day, what all guys really want is a stand-in for their mom."

"…"

Hearing what Lyrule had done took Ringo's breath away. While she disliked admitting it, the young genius inventor had to concede that Lyrule was amazing. Bold, too. If their places had been reversed, Ringo doubted she would've been able to do the same. Mostly likely, she would've simply waited until things died down. She certainly wouldn't have had the courage to force her way into Tsukasa's heart like Lyrule had.

There was no way. Based on Lyrule's actions, Ringo could tell just how serious the elf was about Tsukasa.

"Oh…no…"

Ringo's expression clouded over as she realized how fearsome her rival was. To her, it seemed impossible to win against someone so cheerful, cute, and considerate. Just thinking about it filled Ringo's heart with despair.

That was when Shinobu cheerfully cut in again. "Don't you start worrying, Ringo! Leave it to me! I like Lyrule plenty, too, but…I know how you've been pinin' after Tsukes since middle school."

"_____"

"I'm on your side here, so I'm gonna teach you some secret kunoichi moves to bring your love to fruition!"

Upon hearing her friend's words of reassurance, Ringo realized something. She might not be able to hold a candle to Lyrule when it came to cheerfulness or feminine charm, but Ringo was the leader when it came to strength of feelings.

The girl hadn't given up before, and she wasn't about to do so now. It was for that reason that she'd summoned her courage and asked her friends for help in the first place, after all.

"Th-thank you!" Ringo exclaimed.

Once again, she reaffirmed her conviction. The date was two days away. By the time it arrived...

I'll become...a love-huntress.

Finally, the day of their date rolled around.

Save for a few scattered clouds, the sky was clear and blue. In fact, it hadn't snowed at all in Dormundt over the past few weeks. Perhaps that'd been some sort of aftereffect from Gustav's Rage Soleil war magic. It wasn't exactly something to be applauded, but Ringo was thankful for it just for that day.

The morning was mild, like an Indian summer. Tsukasa and Ringo had agreed to meet up by the bronze statue of Count Heiseraat the First, and Tsukasa had shown up twenty minutes early.

As for Ringo—

"Tsukasa..."

—she was lurking out of sight, watching him from a distance.

It wasn't because she'd misremembered the rendezvous location, though.

Always arrive to a date before the guy, but only go to the meeting spot after he shows up.

According to Shinobu, if you tried to show up a little late from the get-go, you ran the risk of running into trouble and being *seriously* late. Unfortunately, waiting around for a guy wasn't an attractive look, either.

Ringo was putting that lesson into practice. She didn't really understand why it was important, but that didn't matter. It was showtime, and her target was in sight. She was going for the kill today, as a love-huntress.

Still lurking out of sight, Ringo readied her heart, extended her index finger and thumb into the shape of a gun, and pointed at the boy waiting for her by the bronze statue.

"Bang."

"Ah, Ringo. There you are."

"Hwa-wh-wh—*kaff, koff*?!?!"

Their eyes met at the worst possible moment, and Ringo lapsed into a coughing fit.

Worried, Tsukasa rushed over to her.

"Is everything okay? Your face is beet red."

"I-i-i-i-it's fine; everything's all right."

"Are you sure? You aren't sick, are you?"

"N-nope. A-a-all good."

"Really? Well, I'm glad to hear it. Don't push yourself, okay?"

"Y-yeah. I know."

"Very good."

Tsukasa withdrew his silver pocket watch and checked the time.

"It's a bit earlier than planned, but what do you say about lunch? Do you still want to check out that place you messaged me about?"

"Yeah…"

"Then, shall we get going?" With that, Tsukasa sauntered off.

©Sacraneco

After making sure that he'd finally taken his gaze off her, Ringo breathed a deep sigh of relief.

That was close.

If he'd insisted that they head over to Keine to get Ringo checked out, the plan she and Shinobu had painstakingly crafted would've all gone to waste. That danger was in the past now.

While the meetup hadn't gone exactly as Ringo had hoped, things were still on track. The real hunt was just getting started. After getting her head back in the game, she rushed after Tsukasa.

Unfortunately…

"Ah! Angel, sir!"

"Why, if it isn't the angels! Lovely weather today, no?"

"Congratulations on your successful advance into Buchwald and Archride!"

Tsukasa's and Ringo's outfits simply stood out too much. People called to the pair from every direction as they walked the street. It didn't feel like a romantic outing in the slightest.

What can I do…? Ringo panicked. She was finally on a date with Tsukasa, but at this rate, the whole day was going to slip away from them while they were exchanging pleasantries with the townsfolk. That would be a complete waste. A travesty.

Unbeknownst to Ringo, Tsukasa actually felt much the same way.

"…We'll hardly be able to enjoy the rest and relaxation we were prescribed like this, will we?"

While his reasons may have been different, Tsukasa's matter of concern was identical. He wanted to spend the day leisurely relaxing with Ringo, too.

"I did anticipate that this might happen, though, so I have an idea. Follow me."

Tsukasa turned off the path to the restaurant they'd planned on eating at, and he led Ringo to a shop.

More specifically…

"A…clothing store?"

Their destination, apparently, was a secondhand clothing shop in the Industrial District.

"That's right. Our usual outfits are too recognizable, so I thought we might change into something more common in this world. Hopefully, we'll draw less attention that way."

"I…I see."

It was a clever idea.

Ringo agreed, and the two of them headed inside together.

A bell hanging from the door chimed to announce their arrival, and a dark-haired, middle-aged *hyuma* shopkeeper emerged from the back.

"Welcome to— Oh my! Mr. Tsukasa! And Ms. Ringo! What might two angels of the Seven Luminaries want with my humble second-hand shop?"

"Ringo and I have the day off, but our current attire is a bit too conspicuous to go casually sightseeing in. We were hoping to pick up something a little more contemporary." Tsukasa succinctly summed up the situation, and the shopkeeper nodded.

"Ah, I see. That makes perfect sense. Well, if it's clothes you need, then I'm happy to be of service. Right this way." The man led the two toward the back of the store.

Its inventory boasted all sorts of garments, from commoner hand-me-downs to noble garb.

"Many former nobles who lost income to God Akatsuki's reforms sold off much of their wardrobes, so I'm quite proud of my selection at the moment."

"I was thinking of going with something that pairs well with whatever Ringo picks out. Ringo, is there anything that catches your eye?"

"Oh... Um..."

Ringo glanced over the assorted outfits, then pointed to one.

"I—I...kind of...want to try that on..."

"Oh, interesting. It's a different color, but it's pretty similar to what Lyrule wears."

Tsukasa was right. The item Ringo had picked out resembled Lyrule's standard attire. It was a dress comparable to an Austrian dirndl.

Whenever Ringo looked at Lyrule, she was always a little envious of how cute the other girl was dressed. Now that Ringo had a chance, she really wanted to try that sort of clothing on for herself.

The shopkeeper picked up the piece that Ringo had selected. "Ah, this here is a traditional outfit that common-born women of this region wear before they get married. We also have the apparel that noble young ladies wear—are you certain that this is the one you want?"

"Ah, um..."

When the man offered Ringo another option, she stumbled over her answer. Every time she went into clothing stores, the employees would end up launching into gallant sales pitches. Invariably, it always ended poorly for the genius inventor.

Due to her trouble with social situations, Ringo had a habit of getting caught in a salesman's momentum and was easily pressured into buying things she didn't even want. That was why she'd previously done all her shopping online.

However, that sort of convenience didn't exist in this world. She looked desperately to Tsukasa for help. The young politician's response was immediate.

"The original dress is fine, thank you."

Hearing Tsukasa's definitive tone, the shopkeeper gave a slight bow.

"Of course, sir. Eda, come here!"

"On my way, Dad, what's— Whoa! Angels?!"

The dark-haired, rabbit-eared *byuma* girl who emerged from the back of the shop reacted with just as much shock as her father.

"What're two angels doing in our shop?"

"They were hoping to enjoy some privacy on their day off, so they came for a change of garments."

"Ooh, makes sense. Outfits like theirs are pretty unusual for these parts, so it's no wonder they draw so much attention."

"Now, could you take Ms. Ringo and help her try on this dress?"

"G-got it! Please, Ms. Ringo, follow me."

"Oh…"

Ringo hesitated for a moment, not wanting to be separated from Tsukasa in an unfamiliar place. She wasn't about to let him peek at her getting changed, either. Obediently, Ringo followed Eda into the women's changing room.

Next, it was Tsukasa's turn.

"Now, would you mind finding me something that would look natural paired with Ringo's?"

"Of course, sir. Right this way, if you please."

After picking out an outfit with the shopkeeper, he headed for the men's changing room.

"Is it to your liking, Ms. Ringo?"

"W-wow…"

As Ringo looked at her new outfit in Eda's tin mirror, a pleased murmur escaped her lips.

Dressed up in the red-and-white dirndl-style dress, she looked like a dwarf from right out of a fairy tale.

"The corset okay? It's not too tight?"

Nod, nod.

"Thank goodness. And if I may, Ms. Ringo, you look very charming."

"…"

Hearing someone else say that was somewhat embarrassing. Secretly, though, Ringo didn't think she looked half bad, either. What she really wanted was for Tsukasa to see her in it.

Perhaps, if she was lucky, he'd even compliment her appearance.

If he said that…it'd make me super happy.

Heart now racing, Ringo followed Eda out of the changing room.

"Oh, are you finished, too, Ringo?"

Outside, Tsukasa was waiting for her in an aristocratic outfit with gold trim and fabric so blue it seemed to practically shine.

"Ts-Ts-Tsukasa, y-your outfit…!"

"Dad, c'mon. That's a noble's outfit!" Eda asserted that there was a mismatch between Ringo's and Tsukasa's clothes that would cause them to stand out too much.

It'd seemed that the black-haired man who was the shopkeeper had already taken that into account.

"W-well, yes… See, the thing is, Mr. Tsukasa carries himself too elegantly to pass as a commoner anyway. If anything, having him wear plain garb would make him stand out *more*. Fortunately, though, Ms. Ringo is quite good-looking. If we add this silk scarf to her outfit, I was thinking we could pose them as a low-born girl and a noble who fell in love at first sight…"

As the shopkeeper tried explaining his reasoning to his daughter, Tsukasa turned to Ringo.

"How does it look?"

"Y-you look! So cool!"

Forgetting to keep her voice down, Ringo excitedly voiced her approval. Tsukasa was so stylish that just looking at him made the girl dizzy.

Between the way the stark blue outfit set off his dignified silvery hair and the regal posture with which he wore it, he was the spitting image of a fairy-tale prince.

I—I can't even… Being able to see this alone made the hunt worth it…!

Ringo had to carry herself carefully. Satisfying herself merely with seeing Tsukasa in that outfit wasn't what she'd come to achieve.

Tsukasa gave Ringo a rare, unguarded smile, the kind he only showed to those he trusted.

"Thank you. You look pretty adorable yourself."

"Ahhh…!" Ringo's temperature shot up a good five degrees.

He complimented me. Tsukasa called me adorable. Is it really all right for a single day to be so wonderful? The whole thing felt too good to be true. Ringo thought she might go crazy.

When he saw her expression soften, Tsukasa called over to the shopkeeper. "Ringo seems to like it, too, so I think I will go with this one."

"Th-thank you for your patronage! A-although there is one thing I should mention."

"What might that be?"

"I was talking with my daughter, and we were both concerned that, due to how good-looking you both are, the outfits alone might not be enough to avert the public eye."

"So that's where these come in! What do you think?!" Eda handed something to Tsukasa as she spoke. It was a headband with a pair of white wolf ears on it.

"What is it?"

"*Byuma*-ear headbands, a new product I thought up. The idea is that wearing one of these beauties will make you and your *byuma* lover closer than ever!"

"I see. So you're suggesting we go for a fundamental makeover." Tsukasa nodded in thought.

Having a *hyuma* father and a *byuma* mother must have put Eda in a unique position to think such an item up.

"That might not be a bad idea," agreed Tsukasa. "Let's see here…"

After putting the wolf-ear headband on, he turned to Ringo.

"What do you think, Ringo?"

"!!!!!!!!!!!!!!!!"

Immediately, the girl was forced to put her hands over her mouth for fear of letting out a cry of joy. While she did succeed in containing her voice, she failed at restraining the glee that was plain on her expression.

Ringo made sure to soak in the sight, forgetting even to breathe.

Th-the perfect fusion of cool and cute, it's…it's too much to handle!

Somehow, Ringo needed to find a way to preserve this image of him. She wondered if perhaps there was a way to make Tsukasa forget what species he was so he'd leave the ears on for the rest of his life.

Maybe, if I build some sort of brainwashing device…

All it took was a few seconds for Ringo's considerable intellect to arrive at some very alarming places.

"Hmm… Maybe not, then." Tsukasa, having mistaken Ringo's wordless elation for rejection, made to take the headband off. The moment he raised his hand toward his head, though, Ringo grabbed it to stop him. It was an impressive leaping catch—and a reasonably forceful one, at that.

Given Ringo's personality, Tsukasa was surprised that she would do something so aggressive.

"I-it looks…really good! It looks good, so…don't…take it off!"

"Are…are you sure?"

Nod, nod, nod, nod, nod, nod, nod!

As Ringo jerked her head up and down vigorously, she cast a reproachful gaze at him for even thinking about removing the headband.

Tsukasa turned to the shopkeeper's daughter.

"Well then, miss, it looks like I'll be taking this headband. Would you mind getting us one that matches Ringo's hair, too?"

"Of course! Pleasure doin' business!"

When the pair of Prodigies left the shop, both appeared to be *byuma*.

"Looks like we're not drawing quite so much attention now. I can still sense a few people staring but not enough to concern ourselves over."

"Y-yeah, you're right."

Having arranged for their Earth clothes to be sent back to their respective residences, Tsukasa and Ringo resumed their walk to the restaurant.

There were unmistakably fewer stares.

Apparently, *byuma* versus *hyuma* was a big part of how folks in this world distinguished between people, so nobody realized that the two of them were actually Tsukasa and Ringo.

In a sense, they'd achieved their goal. There was one type of look they were actually attracting *more* of, however.

"Wh-who's that *byuma* hottie?!"

"Have we always had a noble like that around these parts?!"

"Go try hitting on him, honey."

"N-no way! If I tried talking to someone that handsome, my heart'd stop!"

Local girls were severely lusting after Tsukasa.

Dressed as he was in his aristocrat's outfit, Tsukasa was turning the head of every woman they passed by. Ringo wasn't surprised, though.

Tsukasa was short and slender for a man. Doubtless, many would've believed him to be a somewhat masculine woman. Unlike Akatsuki, however, who people *only* saw as a girl, Tsukasa had an unmistakable androgynous charm to him. Between that, his snow-white hair, and his heterochromatic red and blue eyes, he carried a certain mystique.

He was less *handsome* and more *beautiful.*

When someone with looks like that wore an outfit that looked like it belonged on a fairy-tale prince, it was only natural that he garnered attention.

Am I...even worthy of walking by his side...?

The weight of the passionate gazes being directed Tsukasa's way made Ringo start to feel self-aware.

No matter how you looked at it, her appearance was clearly just that of a forgettable village girl. Ringo began to wonder if it wasn't the height of conceit for someone like her to not only go on a date with one so fair but to try and take his heart for her own.

As feelings of inadequacy began to pile on poor Ringo, her pace began to slow. Curiously, even after her speed had lagged several times over, her position at Tsukasa's side never changed. Ringo immediately realized what was happening; Tsukasa was nonchalantly matching her pace.

The girl looked up, but Tsukasa pretended not to have noticed anything, merely asking, "What's up?"

Such thoughtfulness and consideration sent a pang of warmth through Ringo's heart.

Tsukasa's so kind... That was something Ringo already knew full well, however. It was that gentleness that'd saved her and made her fall for him.

I can't...give up. Ringo shut her eyes tight.

"*Listen, 'kay? Like I said, love is like hunting.*"

"*Hunting...?*"

"*Yup. So you can't just look at your prey from afar. Unless you make a move, you're just bird-watching. If you wanna catch the bluebird of happiness for yourself, you can't just stare up at the sky. You gotta take aim, pull the trigger, and tell yourself you're gonna shoot it down!*"

"*I'm gonna shoot it down...?*"

"*Put your heart into it! 'I'm gonna shoot it down!'*"

"*I-I'm gonna shoot it down!*"

"*Yeah!*"

"*Y-yeah!*"

Thinking back on what Shinobu had taught her helped Ringo find her confidence again.

That's right. Today, I'm the love-huntress.

Ringo had no intention of going home empty-handed. She'd come to hunt!

I have to be patient, though. I need to start by slowly closing the gap bit by bit.

Step one in that process was...

"*Step one! While walkin', casually hold his hand!*"

"*N-no way, I can't...*"

"*Sure you can! I mean, this is the basic of the basics. If you can't pull this off, the rest is gonna be impossible.*"

"*B-but...*"

"*If tellin' him that you wanna hold hands is too hard, you can pretend to trip and grab on to his arm. If you do that, Tsukes'll probably take your hand outta consideration. But no matter who initiates, you gotta make absolutely sure to interlock fingers with him. You wanna be holding hands like a pair of lovers, not like a dad and his kid. That way, you're showin' him how you feel."*

According to Shinobu's *kunoichi* teachings, demonstrating affection was key. One couldn't expect the other party to be psychic, after all.

"Isn't that too blatant?"

"That's the point—if you aren't so proactive that it makes you a little uncomfortable, he won't know that you see him as anything more than a friend."

Apparently, getting the message "I like you romantically" across was crucial.

While that certainly made sense—

"Pant... Pant..."

—when Ringo tried to put that plan into action, she realized just how high of a hurdle it was.

It wasn't enough just to hold hands with Tsukasa, but she also had to do so with her fingers interlocked with his, like lovers.

Wh-what should I do...? I mean, this is...this is really lewd!

Ringo herself had recently thought that holding hands was no big deal, but now that she was looking at Tsukasa's hand and actually picturing it, it seemed so overwhelming.

His fingers, sliding against hers. All ten of them, together in a line!

When Ringo imagined the sensation, her blood pressure skyrocketed. Trying to go through with it made the girl feel like something in her brain was going to pop.

She couldn't bring herself to take that first step. The most she could do was breathe heavily as she snatched glances at Tsukasa's hand. That was precisely why it was so important that Ringo pressed on, however.

It's like...Shinobu said...

If Ringo couldn't manage this much, the rest was impossible. Shinobu had been right on the mark. Ringo wanted to be in a relationship with Tsukasa. To do that, she would eventually need to express her feelings clearly.

If she couldn't even fake an accident and grab his hand, how was she ever going to be able to get anywhere? With a large inhale, Ringo put her plan into action.

"'E-eeek…'" While her delivery was a bit monotone, Ringo leaned toward Tsukasa just like Shinobu had taught her and grabbed on to his arm with both hands.

"Careful there. Are you okay, Ringo?"

"I—I—I—I—I just d-d-d-d-didn't want to bump into you…" Steam was practically billowing from the poor girl's head, but she tried desperately to keep her cool.

"Oh, good thinking. The road is narrow, and there certainly are a lot of people coming and going."

Much to Ringo's dismay, Tsukasa didn't offer her his hand, however.

"But now, that won't be a problem."

"…Huh?"

"We're here."

"…"

Ringo had been utterly transfixed on Tsukasa's arm, but when she looked up, she saw the lunchtime crowd bustling inside an old wooden building.

The sign on its door, written in the local language—Altan—read PINOT NOIR.

This was the restaurant Ringo had learned about from Shinobu and had suggested to Tsukasa.

"This is the place, right? The restaurant you said you wanted to go to?" asked Tsukasa.

"Ah, uh, yes...it is," Ringo replied.

"We should go in, then. Getting here took longer than planned, so I'm famished."

With that, Tsukasa entered and announced they had a party of two. Ringo just stared at his back.

"*Sniff...*"

She felt like crying. After reminding herself that things weren't over yet, she shook her head to clear her mind.

It's okay... I tried my hardest...

At the very least, Ringo had given an effort instead of conceding without doing anything. She'd fought through her bashfulness and taken action. Even though she ended up losing to the clock, what was important was that she'd tried.

In that moment, Ringo graduated from being the girl gazing at her loved one from afar. Now she was a full-fledged love-huntress. That meant she was just getting started. It was time to get serious.

With little clenched fists, Ringo followed Tsukasa into the restaurant.

"*Step two! Set up a little incident to close the distance between your hearts!*"

"*Set up...an incident?*"

"*Yeah! Just 'cause you're on a date doesn't mean exciting stuff's gonna happen on its own. If you aren't proactive, you might just end up eating and hanging out. Kind of a waste, don'cha think? To prevent that, you wanna set something up on purpose.*"

"*L-like what?*"

"*Good question! For first dates, I like to set up something big and flashy so I can strut my stuff and really sweep the guy off his feet, but that's probably not how you're gonna wanna play it. Something cutesy'd fit you better... All right, I've got it. During lunch, you're gonna snatch an indirect kiss!"*

"A-a-an indirect kiss..."

"Yup. First, you wanna pick out the restaurant the day before. I'd go with Pinot Noir in the Industrial District. The food's great, but more importantly, all the tables get filled up with workers from the glass workshop nearby, so it forces you to sit at the counter. That bit's key. Listen close, Ringo—even if there is a table open, you hafta get a seat at the counter anyway. Then you sit down on Tsukes's dominant side, to his right."

"But...why?"

"If you sit across from him, it'll be harder to pretend you took his cup on accident. It'd be weird to grab it from all the way across the table, right? But at a counter, it's easy to make it look natural. And you're ambidextrous, so even better. Then, after you get the indirect kiss, make sure he finds out. Once he does, Tsukes'll say somethin' like, 'Oh, I'm sorry. I must have put it down too close to you. Here, let me get you a fresh cup.' That's where you smile and go, 'I don't mind...since it's yours.' Lemme tell you, guys go crazy for stuff like that!"

Just as planned, the two of them were seated at Pinot Noir's counter. Sitting on Tsukasa's right, Ringo recalled more of the advice she'd received from Shinobu.

Shinobu is amazing... Ringo never would've come up with the idea to intentionally plan something like that—not in a million years. Ringo was grateful she'd gone to her friend for guidance.

"Here are your orders!" A cat-eared waitress arrived with their food.

Tsukasa's meal consisted of cheese, bread, and stew. Ringo, however, had paired her bread with three sausages and a fried egg. She was generally a light eater, so having meat for lunch was a bit out of character for her.

It's fine. Today, I'm a huntress. A predator!

Perhaps it was sort of her version of a good-luck charm.

Then, at long last, their drinks arrived. Ringo had made sure to order the same thing as Tsukasa, of course. Even if they'd been switched, one would've never been able to know by the contents. Both had been poured in copper cups of identical make, too. Just like Shinobu had said, Ringo wouldn't be running into any problems in that regard.

Ringo lifted her cup to her mouth, hid her expression behind it, and waited for her chance while surrounded by her drink's wheat-like aroma. Like a lioness lurking in the coppery thicket for an opportunity to attack her prey, Ringo waited.

At last, Tsukasa lifted his cup, drank down about a third of his ale, and put it back on the counter.

There. The hunt is on…!

Without a moment's delay, Ringo leaped into action. Placing her own drink down, she prepared to "accidentally" snatch her prey's cup.

W-wait, hold up…!

At the last moment, Ringo realized she'd made an unfortunate mistake.

If she put down her cup and immediately picked Tsukasa's up, there was no way it'd pass as a mistake. The fact that a late bloomer like Ringo was on the offensive was commendable, but even she knew the importance of not playing things too hastily.

Ringo took a moment to compose herself, then took a bite of her sausage. After chewing for an appropriate amount of time, she reached once more for Tsukasa's cup.

That's when it happened.

A cup was lifted into the air, but it wasn't Tsukasa's. It was Ringo's, the one she'd just put down. What's more, the hand that was lifting it belonged to Tsukasa.

What...? Ringo wouldn't have believed it had she not seen it with her own two eyes.

Tsukasa's lips made contact with the bit still wet with Ringo's own saliva.

"Glug, glug..."

Then he ran his upper lip over his lower lip and licked her saliva clean off it. That one moment felt like it lasted an eternity.

Ringo had been prepared to experience an indirect kiss herself, but receiving one was an entirely different matter. She'd never considered such a possibility.

Her spit had touched his lips, and he'd licked it up.

The shock sent anxious thoughts shooting through Ringo's brain one after another, like a computer bombarded with malignant pop-up ads.

It didn't taste weird, did it? It didn't smell funny? What did I have to eat yesterday?

"Mmm, delicious. This restaurant you suggested is nice. I'll have to...hmm? What's wrong? Is there something on my face?"

"Ah-hwah... Fwah."

Ringo fainted and collapsed.

"Wh— R-Ringo?! Are you okay?!"

"Bweh..."

"Your face is red, and you're burning up! You really are ill, then? Ringo, can you hear me?! Ringooooo?!"

"O Juleo, Juleo! Wherefore are you Juleo?"

"That voice, like a goddess's harp! Could it be Romiet?"

"Juleo, discard your family name! And for that name, which is no part of you, take all myself!"

"I take you at your word! I take all of you! And in turn, I offer you all of me! I stand before you as nothing but your Juleo!"

H-how shameful...

She hadn't just made trouble for Tsukasa but everyone in the restaurant.

Mortified, Ringo wanted to crawl into a hole and disappear. Dragging her heels forever wouldn't do, however. There was still one hope that rallied her flagging spirit. The plan had already moved onto its next phase.

"Then, step three, the clincher! Appreciation of the performing arts!"

"P-performing arts?"

"Yeah! Dormundt's where all the nobles in Findolph gather, so it's got all sorts of places for leisure activities. Notably, a theater. A bunch of the nobles use it as a date spot, so most of what they put on are love stories. The building has a big hall, and when plays are going on, they shut all the windows and only use stage lighting. It makes it almost feel like a movie theater."

"Isn't that...kind of cliché, for a date?"

"Hey, they call it tried-and-true for a reason. If it ain't broke, don't fix it. Once you're there, you only have one mission—gently hold his hand and look into his eyes."

"Without...talking?"

"Of course. C'mon, Ringo, talkin' during a play is bad manners. If you look at it another way, though, theaters are nice because they let you get away with not talking. You don't hafta worry about thinkin' of anything fancy to say.

"When the characters' romance starts getting heated, you just lay your hand atop your guy's and look into his eyes. Then, focus every 'I

love you!' you can—'Je t'aime!' 'Wŏ ài nǐ!'—*into your gaze and shoot 'im down!"*

Gaze at him with every "I love you" you can.

This time, Ringo didn't have to entwine fingers like lovers, nor did any of their mucous membranes need to touch. All she had to do was put her hand on Tsukasa's and look at him. Even she could do that.

While Ringo had no confidence in her looks or her figure, the one thing she was certain of was her love for Tsukasa.

I can do it, she told herself as she waited for the performance's climax. Shinobu had coached her on the plot ahead of time. Apparently, the two lead characters were supposed to share a kiss near the end of the play. It was in that moment that Ringo would tell Tsukasa how she felt. Not with words, of course, but with her eyes.

At last, she'd lay plain her feelings for him. She'd finally convey all the things she'd kept hidden ever since that one evening in middle school when she'd spotted him in the shopping district.

All the love would pour from her heart.

That had been the plan, at least.

"It felt almost like I'd seen that before somewhere, but it was all so dramatic and fantastical that I found myself enjoying it anyway."

Ringo nodded in agreement, tears of emotion streaming down her cheeks as she gave the performers a round of applause. Her clapping had a dejected sort of energy to it, however.

The play had been compelling, it really had. Unfortunately, that had been the problem.

...I got so into it, I couldn't tear my eyes from the stage...

At that moment, Ringo realized something—she was the same way with her research. Whenever she got focused on work, everything else melted away. Perhaps her romantic theater visit plan had been a dud from the get-go.

After the performance, Tsukasa and Ringo made their way to a park. As thanks for suggesting the nice lunch spot, Tsukasa had offered to treat Ringo to black tea and dried apples from the park's concession stand. When the pair arrived, he had her save seats on a bench while he went and got the food. Ringo watched Tsukasa go, then heaved a heavy sigh.

"Haaah…"

She'd botched each and every one of the tricks Shinobu had taught her. Today, the lioness was going home hungry. In fact, she probably wasn't even a lion; Ringo now thought of herself as closer to a tawny little house cat.

Sitting there alone, Ringo compared herself to the heroine from the play.

Romiet was incredible.

First, she'd murdered to avenge her friend. Then, when her beloved Juleo was run out of town, she got some poison from a servant and used it to kill every last member of her and Juleo's feuding families, as they'd been the ones who had prevented the two lovers from getting married.

Now *there* was a strong woman. Maybe too strong, actually, but even that was better than being weak. Better forceful than meek when it came to getting what the heart wanted. In the end, it seemed that women really had to be proactive, too, like Romiet.

Ringo lamented her helplessness.

"…"

Now that all her plans had failed, the tension fueling her was draining away, and a wave of fatigue washed over the girl.

She'd spent all last night running through mental simulations in preparation for the date, so she'd barely gotten any sleep. Giving in to the drowsiness, Ringo drifted off into dreamland.

It was a light sleep and an old dream.

A dream of childhood.

I, Ringo Oohoshi, am not a normal human. Not in terms of talent but in terms of the process by which I was created.

My mother, Dr. Juri Oohoshi, created me by combining a gene-edited sperm and ovum. Although she was the one who carried me to term, my genetic makeup didn't correspond to that of any particular human.

In other words, I was a *manufactured genius*.

As a product of my mother's research results, my intelligence began showing itself at a very young age. I understood arithmetic before I could walk. I mastered three languages before I was weened.

By age seven, I already held several patents for my inventions, including the "All-Purpose Gloves" said to have doubled the world's productivity.

I quickly became obsessed with inventing. While it was undoubtedly fun in and of itself, my primary motivator was how happy it made my mother. Bringing her joy thrilled me in return. We might not have been connected by blood, but our hearts were linked all the same. Believing that, I worked hard to please her.

At some point, though…she stopped lavishing praise on me. After thinking about why, I came to the conclusion that my efforts must have been lacking in some way. So I started working harder than ever.

I studied, researched, and created new technologies and machines. Eventually, I created "Ultra-Performance Solar Panels" that were a thousand times more efficient than the conventional type. I concocted "Liquid Metal" that could alter its molecular structure in response to electrical signals and freely change its shape. I developed the "RM Method," a way to solidify radioactive matter and prevent it from generating radioactive waste. I devised a way to digitize a person's memories and personality completely, and all of those were just the tip of the iceberg when it came to my accomplishments.

Around the time I'd turned twelve, everyone was telling me I'd advanced human civilization by five centuries.

But…the only person I actually wanted praise from, my mother, didn't say so much as a single kind word.

I was at a loss.

Utterly flummoxed, I eventually went and asked her. Was there anything she wanted me to do? Perhaps she wanted something from me? No matter the request, I was ready to make it a reality.

That's when it happened.

For the first time in my life…my mother hit me. I can still remember exactly what she said afterward, and her cold voice still rings in my ears at times.

"You'll do anything, huh? Yeah, I bet you will. Everything's so easy for you, isn't it? We humans must look like knuckle-dragging idiots to you, right? Must be nice, looking down on us. You're not even human, you fake…you monster!"

…I don't like to think about the year that followed.

Day after day, my mother would say and do horrible things to me. She started with punching and kicking, but with each day, the violence escalated. I didn't understand why she was doing it.

All I understood was that if she was angry, it must've somehow been my fault. Clearly, I had made some kind of mistake.

So I endured.

Once the long, long punishment was over, I was certain she'd go back to the kind mother I'd once known. That was the sole hope I clung to. Things didn't play out that way, however.

What ended up saving me wasn't the return of my mother's kindness—it was Japanese civil services. After I suddenly stopped appearing in public, members of an academic association got concerned about my mother's behavior and reported her to the appropriate authorities. When the police saw the abuse she'd been inflicting on me, they immediately apprehended her.

"You should never have been born."

Those were the final words my mother, Juri Oohoshi, ever said to me.

Upon hearing that, I finally understood what the problem was. My mother…was jealous of me—and afraid. She was afraid that her daughter, who'd exceeded her wildest expectations time and time again, would render her existence worthless.

Worse still, her fears were legitimate.

By that point, there wasn't a single thing that Juri Oohoshi could do that Ringo Oohoshi couldn't. Once I realized that…I fell into a deep depression. Nothing interested me anymore.

The seasons shifted, and I entered middle school, but nothing changed. I was drifting aimlessly through life like a jellyfish.

The woman who'd created me had rejected my very existence.

Who was I? For what purpose was I even alive?

I didn't know. Without an answer, even the act of thinking started to annoy me.

One day, as I sat in my classroom and stared blankly at the sky, a thought crossed my mind like it was the most obvious thing in the world.

I wondered if I was better off being dead.

That was when—

"Forgive me, but you're Ringo Oohoshi, the genius inventor, right?"

—Tsukasa Mikogami appeared.

Back then he was just some boy in my class who'd randomly started talking to me during break time. I had always been shy, and the incident with my mother had only served to worsen that tendency. I thought it best to simply ignore him.

Undaunted, Tsukasa pressed on anyway and placed something on top of my desk.

"Actually, I have an important favor I wanted to ask of you."

It was a silver pocket watch. Tsukasa motioned to it as he spoke.

"It seems to be broken. Even when I wind it up, the hands don't turn."

"………"

So what? I thought.

"I'd like you to repair it."

"………?!"

Honestly, I glowered at him. Who did this guy think he was, coming up and demanding things of me?

"Should be a simple task for an inventor of your caliber, right?"

That much was true. It probably wouldn't have even taken ten minutes. I could've had it done before the next class started.

What I wanted to know was, why did I have to?

"Please. It was a birthday gift from my father, and it means a lot to me."

"………………"

Awkward as I was, I couldn't bring myself to voice my objections. Overwhelmed, I gave up and agreed to fix the watch. I assumed that the sooner I got it done, the sooner I'd be rid of him.

Bringing the little thing home, I went into my workshop for the first time in a year and made the necessary repairs. The watch wasn't in the best shape, so it took a little longer than I'd expected, but in the end, I successfully got it working again.

The next day, I returned it to him.

"Thanks, you're a lifesaver."

No sooner had he thanked me than—

"And a beautiful job done, at that. You really seem to have a knack for this stuff. Given your skill, I think you'd be able to fix this MP3 player, too."

"...?!"

—he made another outrageous request.

"I'm counting on you."

In the end, I caved to the pressure and accepted. It didn't stop after that second repair job, either. Whenever I finished one of his requests, he'd just make another one ad infinitum.

I was taken aback and had to wonder if this Tsukasa had no shame. My social anxieties kept me from refusing, however. Reluctantly, I fulfilled every one of his demands.

Sometimes, I didn't have the tools or parts necessary, and other times, I didn't know how to fix whatever it was and had to learn from scratch. For example, there was one time Tsukasa brought a speaker for me to restore.

It was set up in such a way that the speaker's material and the construction of its frame allowed for fine control of the audio output. Fixing the inner components alone wasn't enough to rebuild it.

I used one of my old connections to get in touch with the manufacturer, but that was only the first step. Even once they sent me the frequency response data, many of the speaker's parts were out of production, so I had to re-create them myself.

It was a lot of work, but I was so engrossed in it that I started having *fun*. Each new thing I learned only piqued my curiosity more. My mind teemed with countless blueprints.

I'd sworn not to invent anymore. My mother was gone, and she was never going to praise me again, so I'd assumed there was no point.

That hadn't been true, however.

For the first time in my life, I realized that I *liked* inventing things. Upon that discovery, it was like the floodgates had opened. There were so many things I wanted to make, so many things I wanted to try. Wasting my time on someone else's problems wasn't how I wanted to spend my life.

So I summoned up all my courage and turned down the boy's incessant stream of requests.

It was probably the first time in my life I had ever told someone "No." In all honesty, I was terrified. I couldn't help but wonder if he was going to get angry or even attack me.

To my surprise, however—

"*I see.* I'm glad to hear it."

"…?"

—the expression of joy that crossed his face when I refused his request put the one he'd shown when I fixed his pocket watch to shame.

Why is he making that face? Why is he glad that I refused his demand?

At the time, I hadn't understood.

That same evening, though…things changed. I was planning on holing up in my laboratory for the first time in ages, so I made a rare trip to the local shopping district to stock up on supplies. There, by happenstance, I spotted him.

He was carting a wagon full of junk around, returning it to the neighborhood's residents, and apologizing. One of the items was the radio-cassette player he'd asked me to fix that day. I wasn't always quick on the uptake, but even I could tell what was going on.

All that time, I'd thought he was being selfish. I'd known that Tsukasa was a politician's son, and his actions had just served to enforce my prejudices.

That hadn't been it at all. Tsukasa hadn't been doing it for himself. He hadn't even been doing it for them.

"I'm glad to hear it."

Day in and day out, he'd been going around the town and collecting junk for me. He saw me fading away, and he wanted to stop me from vanishing. When I realized just how kind he was, a new sort of pain struck my heart.

It shot through me like a bolt of lightning and was stronger than anything I'd ever felt before.

In all likelihood, that was the moment when I, Ringo Oohoshi, fell in love with Tsukasa Mikogami.

"Huuhn…"

Rousing gently from her nostalgic dream, Ringo returned to the waking world. The time had come for her nap to end. She did as her body instructed and opened her eyelids.

"You awake?"

"Tsu…kasa…?"

When she looked up, the first thing she saw was Tsukasa's mismatched eyes.

As her consciousness gradually returned, Ringo noticed two things.

The first was that she was lying down on the bench with Tsukasa's blue overcoat draped over her as a makeshift blanket. The second was that her head was resting on Tsukasa's lap.

"—?!"

The moment it occurred to Ringo what was going on, she shot straight up.

"Wh-wh-why'm I on your l-lap...?!" She was flummoxed, and her face was downright scarlet.

"Hmm? Oh, that. When I came back with the tea, you were lying down on the bench. Thanks to Rage Soleil, it's warm enough that I didn't have to worry about you catching a cold, and you were resting so peacefully that I didn't want to wake you."

"Huh...?"

Upon hearing that, Ringo finally turned her attention to things besides Tsukasa. That's when she noticed that the sky was cast in a vermillion shade. Taking in that sight, the girl immediately understood what had happened. When she'd dozed off while waiting for Tsukasa, she had actually fallen asleep for several hours.

Now understanding that—

"...Heh, ah-ha-ha."

—Ringo let out a little giggle.

Not only had none of the tricks Shinobu taught her worked, but Ringo had also fallen asleep in the middle of the date. Faced with such a comedy of errors, what other option was there *but* to laugh?

That's not to suggest that Ringo felt defeated, however.

It's all right, though.

She did have a pleasant enough dream. Perhaps it'd even come about because she'd been sleeping while surrounded by Tsukasa's scent.

The nap had reminded her of the moment she first learned of love's sweet pain and its sweet bliss.

Neither before nor after that moment had Ringo ever felt such a powerful pang of emotion. That's why one poor date was nothing to get worked up about. There was always next time.

Tsukasa had been the one to suggest this first date, but all Ringo had to do was take the initiative in the future and ask for another herself.

Not only had Ringo been fortunate enough to meet someone she loved deeply, but right now, he was sitting at her side.

"Hey, um?"

"What's up?"

"Can…we take a…selfie?"

"Dressed like this?"

Ringo nodded emphatically.

"…Sure. Do you want to do the honors?"

"Okay!"

Ringo leaned in close to Tsukasa with a beaming bob of her head and used her smartphone's front-facing camera to snap a shot of them in their lavish outfits. It was sure to become a picture to remember the day.

"Hee-hee… I'll cherish this."

"Would you mind sending it to my phone later?"

"Of course."

Standing up from the bench, Ringo expressed her gratitude to Tsukasa again.

"Thank you…for inviting me today. I had…a lot of fun."

"Yeah, so did I… This was a very productive day off," Tsukasa replied. "It was my first time viewing the city through the eyes of its residents."

As Tsukasa spoke, he looked off into the distance. When Ringo followed his gaze, she saw the High-End Residential District, which was in the midst of being repaired.

Even while Tsukasa and the others had been fighting the

©Sacrane

subjugating army, the reconstruction efforts had been chugging along. The city's people were rebuilding with nothing but their own strength—and to considerable effect, to boot.

They were sweating side by side, helping each other out with no regard to status. Everyone simply considered one another neighbors.

"…This is a fine city," Tsukasa murmured. "The seeds of democracy are finally sprouting in this world. And that's why we need to protect it." The white-haired boy's tone grew firmer with each word.

Picking up on that, Ringo turned her gaze from the High-End Residential District back toward him. Tsukasa was looking right at her, and his eyes burned with resolve.

"To that end, Ringo…there's something I need you to do. It's necessary to protect those seeds, and you're the only one who can do it."

…*Hmm?* Something seemed off about Tsukasa, however.

From his expression and his tone, Ringo could sense that there was something weighing on him. The girl had yet to realize what it was, though. Perhaps dismissing the uncertain feeling as her own imagination, Ringo nodded.

"Please tell me."

That night, when Ringo returned to her lab, Bearabbit came over to greet her.

"*Welcub back, Ringo! How'd the date go?*"

"It was good. I had a really good time."

As she spoke, she showed Bearabbit the picture of her and Tsukasa.

"*Wow, you two are unbearably cute!*"

"Thanks. I'll send it to you later… By the way, Bearabbit…"

"*Hmm?*"

"How far are we on the geological survey of the three domains?"

"About halfway through, but we already found a big gold vein in Buchwald. I told Tsukasa so he's well abear," replied the AI, though not entirely sure what had prompted the inquiry.

"Got it," Ringo answered as she took off her outfit. "I'm going to go take a shower and go to sleep, but if you could have that data up on the server by tomorrow, that'd be great."

"Ringo...?"

As Ringo laid out her uncharacteristically snappy instructions, Bearabbit sensed something was up and glanced at his creator's face.

That's when he saw it.

"Tomorrow, we're starting our biggest job yet, so be ready."

Ringo's expression was grim and brimming with cold determination.

CHAPTER 3

◈ One Who Would Kill God ◈

"Move aside, move aside!"

"Bring in more snow! And fresh cloths!"

"It hurts… I'm burning…"

A massive, blue-roofed mansion sat in western Gustav. The Seven Luminaries owned the building, and it was crammed full with patients and filled with their agonized moans.

One of the doctors had brought Akatsuki and Aoi in, and the two of them gasped upon seeing the condition of the makeshift hospital.

"Yikes, th-things are looking pretty gnarly here…er, I mean, this state of affairs doth displease me."

"We knew that the domain's people were starving, that we did, but…Mash, m'lord, what ailment is it that plagues them so? An epidemic?"

The young *byuma* man who'd taken them there, Mash, answered.

"No, they're all afflicted by miasma."

"Miasma?"

"It's the malevolent energy that fills this world. Unless you treat wounds with alcohol, it invades the body, causing fevers, swelling, and pain. Healthy people can withstand a bit of it, but because of their malnutrition, the Gustav domain's citizens have lost their resistance, and the miasma is eating away at them. Dr. Keine referred to it as *sepsis*, I believe."

"Ah. I'm familiar with that malady, that I am."

Hearing Mash refer to it as *miasma* had stumped them, but it turned out that all he was talking about was bacteria. Aoi had spent much of her life on battlefields, so she was well acquainted with sepsis. It was a serious condition caused by bacteria entering the bloodstream that resulted in inflammation all throughout the body.

"Per Dr. Keine's instructions, we gathered all the sepsis patients together here. It pains me to admit it, but…we're having problems treating them. There are far more of them than we'd anticipated, and there simply isn't enough of the holy water Dr. Keine gave us to go around."

Mash gave Akatsuki a deep bow.

"Please, God Akatsuki, might I ask that you use your miraculous powers to heal our sick?!"

Uh-oh…

When Akatsuki heard Mash's request, he felt stupid for having agreed to come in the first place. Akatsuki was a magician—an illusionist. His miracles, like where he'd flown through the air and made mountains disappear, had all just been stage magic backed by tricks and contrivances. Akatsuki was no more a god than anyone else in the room. In short, he had no way of granting Mash's plea.

At the same time, however, admitting as much was not an option. He understood full well the implications of his current position as the Seven Luminaries' holy figure. Saying anything that would mar his divinity wasn't allowed.

Akatsuki racked his brain as he considered how he was going to get out of this. As his thoughts frantically churned in futility, a new voice cut in.

"Well, well, well. Now, this is a grim spectacle."

Its ridicule-filled tone seemed deeply out of place, given the gravity of the situation. When Akatsuki and Aoi turned to see who it was, they were greeted by a group of five *hyuma*. A well-dressed man with bobbed hair, presumably a noble, seemed to be their leader. He cast a gaze at Akatsuki and the others that was just as scornful as his voice.

"The chorus of shrieks and wails filling this mansion... It's the very portrait of hell, no?"

"Why are you here, Count?"

"'Why,' you ask? Well, the Seven Luminaries banned our Healer Association's nostrum, so I came to see what manner of healing they employ and perhaps learn a thing or two. But *this*... As I see it, they're merely allowing these poor people to suffer. Wouldn't you all agree?" The question was directed at the count's entourage, who made no effort to mince their words.

"Absolutely. They ban our nostrum, the medicine that could save these people from their suffering, and this is the best they can manage? Pathetic!"

"Some god you turned out to be! Ha-ha-ha!"

Aoi arched her eyebrows vigilantly and posed a question to Mash.

"Who are these people?"

"The one in front is Count Selentius...commanding officer of the Blue Brigade's logistics division and chairman of the Healer Association. The other four are all Healer Association members."

Aoi and Akatsuki were familiar with the organization. As the name suggested, it was a group of healers that operated out of the Gustav domain. Tsukasa had arranged to have them help improve health conditions in the region. Yet, for whatever reason...

"They've adopted a rather prickly attitude, that they have."

Mash explained why.

"They bear a grudge over the fact that Dr. Keine banned their nostrum—opium—on account of its addictive, dependence-forming properties. They were in the business of getting patients hooked on the stuff, then wringing everything they could from them. I don't just mean money, either. They took belongings and property, too."

At that point, Count Selentius cut in with an objection.

"I ask that you not spread such slander, eh? I'll admit that patients tend to become dependent on our opium, but it also has the power to free them from their pain. As a doctor yourself, young Mash, surely you understand the salvation that offers, no? Driven mad by fever, skin flushed…these people are beyond saving. They're already in death's clutches. Surely the humane thing to do is offer them a peaceful send-off, is it not?"

"Count! How dare you say that in front of the patients…!" Mash raised his voice in protest at the callous statement. Even though their profession dealt with matters of life and death, there were some things best left unsaid. Before he had a chance to continue his dressing down of Count Selentius, Elch rushed through the hall, his face white as a sheet.

"Hey! Is…? Is Dr. Keine here?! Milinda's in bad shape!"

Akatsuki and the others hurried after Elch into the drawing-room beside the main hall. Inside, a *byuma* girl was gasping in pain atop a bed. It was Milinda, the girl Elch and Shinobu had met in Coconono Village. She, too, was a patient at the manor.

After the lashes she'd received, bacteria had gotten into the wound, and she'd contracted sepsis as well. Evidently, it was severe enough that she'd been allotted one of the few available beds.

"Milinda! Milinda, stay with me!" cried her mother, Emelada.

"Agh… Gah…" The poor girl could only gasp in reply.

"Her fever's gotten worse, and even though her eyes are open, it's like she's just staring off into space. Dr. Keine really isn't here?!" Emelada asked with tears in her eyes.

"I'm terribly sorry. Dr. Keine left this morning, saying she had something important to attend to... For now, it's just me." Having delivered the bad news, Mash began his examination. It didn't take long for his expression to turn grim.

"It's bad. She's starting to lose consciousness, and her limbs have gone pale... This is—"

"Her end is nigh. With symptoms like that, she won't last a week."

"Count!"

Suddenly, a face popped up behind Mash, and Count Selentius spoke with the same unsympathetic tone as before. Mash made no efforts to conceal his contempt for his unwanted, inconsiderate shadow.

"Please, shut up already! You, bring me some holy water, fast!" Mash barked at a nearby nurse.

Dejectedly, the woman replied, "W-we used up the last of it yesterday..."

"Rgh—!"

What they referred to as "holy water" were antibiotics, mainly penicillin, that Keine had produced over in Dormundt. Penicillium mold generated a material with powerful antibacterial qualities. The use of which would likely save Milinda.

Unfortunately, Keine had only just started mass cultivation. As such, there was only so much she could create at a time. Due to the massive influx of patients, they'd burned through her entire stockpile.

"Ma...ma..."

"Milinda, Mom's right here! I'm right here, honey!"

"Mama...where...are you...? It...hurts... It hurts...Mama..."

"Milinda... Oh, God! Please, please save my Milinda! I'm begging you! Please!"

Seeing her daughter without even the strength to speak, Emelada clung to Akatsuki with a look of abject desperation on her face.

The young magician was overcome with an immense wave of guilt. All his laughter and bravado were worthless here. The fact that he was lying to that poor mother made him feel utterly wretched. He wished he could just tell her the truth and be done with it, but he held his tongue. Exposing himself for what he was now would bring no comfort to anyone save himself. It would only succeed in robbing Emelada of her last shred of hope, and it was sure to cause a lot of trouble for Akatsuki's friends.

As the magician sat there pondering…

"Well, well, well, aren't you the heartless deity. You would just leave a poor child to suffer like that?" Selentius leveled a contemptuous quip at Akatsuki and laid his hand atop Emelada's shoulder. With a big smile, he continued.

"Listen, ma'am. Let us give salvation where this cold God won't, eh?"

"Huh?!"

"This opium can take away your girl's pain. It carries a correspondingly high price, but…you're an attractive woman. If you can't afford it, I'm sure we could find you a…*suitable* source of income to pay off the debt." As the count whispered, he pulled a folded, triangular paper pouch of powder from his pocket.

Mash went berserk. "Quit running your mouth! That's enough of your—"

He made to throw Selentius out, but to his surprise, Emelada cut in between them.

"Yes, please! I don't care what happens to me; I'll do anything! Just please, save my girl!" She didn't understand how dangerous opium was. More importantly, however, she couldn't bear to stand by and watch her daughter suffer any longer.

The count merely *smirked* at the despondent woman.

"Can't! That was aaaall a lie."

"Huh…?"

"So very sorry, ma'am. The Seven Luminaries banned the use of our Healer Association's opium, you see. Sooo I'm afraid I can't even prescribe her any. No matter how much you offer to pay, it simply can't be done. Your girl is past rescuing. All that's left for her is an agonizing death as the miasma burns through her body!"

"N-no…!"

"It pains me; it truly does! We would love more than anything to be able to help! So if you want to blame someone, then blame the Seven Luminaries for abandoning these patients and blame their powerless God! Oh-ho-ho-ho!"

Aoi had remained silent but could do so no longer. "I've not run across such a foul, depraved man in quite some time. Shall I silence him for good?"

Her eyes narrowed, and she reached for Hoozukimaru, the katana resting on her waist.

However—

"Restrain yourself, Aoi."

—a dignified voice called her off.

It belonged to prodigy magician Akatsuki. He took a long stride toward the count.

"Listen well, lowly human! When did I claim I couldn't save these people? Never! I'll save the girl, along with every other soul in this building! The angel I've granted the power of healing to, Keine, will bring forth a miracle!"

Admittedly, Akatsuki was being extremely rash. He had no reason to believe Keine could save all those afflicted with sepsis. Such an outlandish promise really wasn't something that God Akatsuki should've said. If any of the patients died, it would be a serious blow to his divinity claims. Even knowing the risk it carried, he had to say it, however.

Akatsuki refused to sit by and watch Selentius trample all over a desperate mother's heart. So he chose to put his faith in Keine Kanzaki.

No sooner had the slight magician made his outrageous declaration, than—

"Quite right, Akatsuki."

—Keine appeared in the doorway and affirmed his statement herself.

"Dr. Keine!"

"…Keine. We meet again, eh?"

Elch and the others reacted to Keine's appearance with joy, while Count Selentius glanced over in her direction with clear disdain. Keine turned her ever-constant smile his way.

"You needn't worry, my good count. I intend to save every last patient here."

In other words, his intervention was unnecessary. The count's lips curled upward.

"Oh-ho-ho…? My, how relieving. But how do you plan to do that, eh? Even I have eyes and ears, and I heard you can only make a tiny amount of your 'holy water' each day. With your stockpile depleted, how do you intend to save all these suffering people? Unless you can squeeze some miracle panacea from stone, you'll never be able to produce enough for all of them."

"Yes, you're quite right. We can't create nearly enough penicillin— holy water, rather—nor can we alleviate these poor people's pain."

"Then, allow us to use our opium to—"

"No. As I said, you needn't worry," Keine interrupted. Before Selentius had time to object again, Keine continued.

*　　*　　*

"I'm going to do exactly what you just suggested. I'm going to squeeze a panacea from rocks."

"...Excuse me?"

Keine walked over to the count, took his hand, and placed something cold and hard in it.

Confused, the man looked down at what he'd been given.

"...Coal?"

"It is indeed...and it's the source of the medicine that will cure these people."

Hearing that, the count's eyes went wide, and he promptly burst into raucous laughter.

"Pfft, ah-ha-ha-ha-ha! This rock emits noxious fumes so foul it can't even be used in the hearth. Even children know that! Mercury is considered a miracle cure, so that would've been one thing, but making medicine out of this common trash? Ah-ha-ha-ha! Now *that* is something else! I suppose you really are an angel! Your ideas are truly unfettered by the common sense of us mortals!"

Selentius enjoyed a few more moments of vulgar revelry before deigning to jeer at Keine again.

"Go on, then. If you think you can make medicine from this junk, be my guest. But when it fails to help anyone...you'll agree to lift the ban on our opium sales. As medical professionals, we refuse to kowtow to you Seven Luminaries while you allow innocent patients to suffer!"

That was the whole reason the count had come to the makeshift hospital that day. He wanted the opium ban lifted under the noble pretense of it being for the sake of the ailing. Keine was well aware of that, but she nodded nonetheless.

"Very well. I have no objections."

"Then it's a promise. Now, allow us to take our leave. Oh-ho-ho-ho!" The count sneered in obvious glee as he left the room.

Mash stared daggers at his back.

"That bastard, talking about helping people when he hasn't done a goddamn thing..."

"Watch your language, Mash," Keine scolded.

"Ah, I'm sorry..."

"Dr. Keine, Milinda is—," Emelada started.

"Yes, I'm aware," Keine interjected.

With the obnoxious man gone, the prodigious doctor got started on Milinda's examination. After looking the infected girl up and down for a moment, Keine withdrew a long needle and pricked Milinda in the neck.

Emelada let out a horrified gasp, but a moment later—

"...Zzz, zzz..."

—the agony in Milinda's expression waned as her breathing stabilized.

"Did her pain...go away?"

"It did. By using a needle to numb her nerves, I was able to dull a good deal of her discomfort."

"Th-thank you, blessed angel!"

Before Emelada could get too excited, however, Keine did her professional due diligence and delivered the bad news.

"Sadly, I've only abated her suffering. Your child's life has not been saved. The bacteria inside her body is still there, so this relief will prove temporary. From what I can see, her symptoms look to be quite advanced. There's no telling when she'll slip into a state of shock. When that happens, her body won't be able to hold out."

"I-it can't be..."

"But know that the human soul is tenacious. It refuses to accept death easily. So as long as her willpower remains strong, her body will be able to hold out for a little while longer. Emelada, I ask that you not give up on your daughter until the bitter end. Hold her hand to bolster her spirit and give us time to prepare medicine for her. She no doubt loves you more than anyone else in the world, making that a task that only you can perform."

"Y-yes. Of course, I will…"

"Very well. Mash, take over for me."

"Yes, ma'am!"

The count had toyed with Emelada's heart nearly to the point of breaking it. Knowing that, Keine left the woman with words of encouragement before putting Mash in charge of the patients and exiting the room with the other two Prodigies to go make the medicine.

As they headed out, Akatsuki turned to Keine with concern in his eyes.

"Hey, Keine. That count guy pissed me off, too, so I get the impressive declaration, but can you really make medicine from coal?"

"But of course," Keine replied with a confident nod. "Although strictly speaking, I'll be using the coal tar that Ringo's coal-powered factory produces as a byproduct."

"C-coal tar?! That nasty, gloopy stuff?!"

"Is such a thing even all right to use on the human body?"

Keine replied to Akatsuki's and Aoi's questions with a smile.

"Mm-hmm. It's common knowledge among medical professionals, but I suppose your reactions are typical for modern youth such as yourselves. However, I'll have you know that coal tar has a long and storied history as a pharmaceutical ingredient. Although we now primarily use steroid ointments in Japan to treat skin diseases, we used topical solutions made from coal tar before they entered the scene. Even today, such solutions are still widely used in the West."

"H-huh. That's kinda surprising, given how dirty it looks."

"Most tend not to be aware of this, but tar has powerful antiseptic properties. That, in turn, means that it's good at preventing the spread of bacteria. Simply put, it's antibacterial. The medicine I'm about to make relies on that quality of coal tar.

"During the wars of the twentieth century, mankind faced off against his longstanding foe, the grim reaper known as sepsis. However, during that era, they took their 'red bullet' and shot it square into the reaper's heart. That 'red bullet' was humanity's first-ever synthetic antibacterial medicine—sulfa drugs."

There existed a branch of science called carbochemistry.

At one point in human history, due to the steam engine's invention and the sky-high price of petroleum gas, humanity began generating huge amounts of coal tar as waste. Naturally, many wanted to find some use for it, if at all possible.

Scholars racked their brains, testing and analyzing that industrial trash every way they could. Finally, they discovered a structure called a benzene ring comprising six carbon atoms arranged in a hexagon. That moment marked the birth of carbochemistry.

Eventually, people learned that they could combine that hexagonal structure with other atoms to create all manner of compounds, both those that existed in the natural world and even those that didn't.

From this revelation came phenol, the cornerstone of antiseptic medicine, aroma compounds that smelled just like cherry blossoms, vivid, nonfading tar dyes, and countless other new creations.

Like the philosopher's stone of legend, that little hexagonal structure was responsible for birthing countless substances, rapidly accelerating mankind's development. Sulfa drugs were merely one of the miracles produced.

"In the 1930s, German pathologist Gerhard Domagk discovered

that a red coal tar dye possessed antibacterial properties and created Prontosil, the very first sulfa drug. With sulfa drugs, mankind now had a way to attack blood-borne pathogens, causing a sharp decline in the mortality rate caused by postsurgical infections. It's said that the drop in surgery-based mortality was directly responsible for the rise in the social status of the medical profession as a whole."

As they walked through the mansion, Keine gave Akatsuki and Aoi a lecture on the history of sulfa drugs. After hearing the history lesson, Akatsuki let out an earnest coo of amazement.

"Wow, I had no idea about any of that."

"Antibiotics like penicillin came onto the scene shortly thereafter and stole the spotlight, so it's only natural that general awareness of them is low. But we doctors won't soon forget the miracle drug that changed the course of medical history."

"Any man who can find antibacterial properties in dye must be quite the incredible fellow, that he must," Aoi praised.

"I should certainly think so. For a German to earn a Nobel Peace Prize shortly after World War Two, he had to be quite incredible indeed. That said, they did discover after the fact that the dye had no antibacterial properties to speak of."

"Huh? Whaddaya mean?"

"In short, thinking that the red dye itself had antibacterial properties was a misconception on Mr. Domagk's part. In truth, those properties belonged to the tar dye they added to their dyes to prevent them from fading. Everyone took its use in dye manufacturing for granted, but that was what afforded the substance its antibacterial effects. The color had nothing to do with it," Keine explained.

"Wait, for real? Even the guy who made it didn't know why it worked?" Akatsuki asked.

"He didn't know the underlying logic, but he did understand that it was effective. It's a relatively common occurrence in the world of medicine. Most pharmaceutical products exist in a constant state of human experimentation. That's why we often discover new, alarming side effects in drugs even after they've been in common use for decades."

"Well, that's not exactly comforting…," muttered Akatsuki.

"I'm afraid I don't quite follow all the technical details, but the long and short of it is that this medicine is capable of saving all these fine people?" Aoi inquired.

"That's right," affirmed Keine.

"Then we should get to work posthaste, that we should. How many hands do you need? I shall assemble them without delay."

Keine shook her head at Aoi's offer.

"Thank you, but that won't be necessary. The synthesis is too dangerous a task to be left to amateurs, and getting people up to speed would take too long."

Synthesizing sulfa drugs wasn't difficult in and of itself. The organic compound that gave them their antibacterial properties, sulfanilamide, had an exceedingly simple molecular structure. Even the facilities and equipment of this more primitive world were sufficient for synthesizing it. The whole reason Keine had chosen sulfa drugs over the comparatively harder-to-produce penicillin was that she eventually planned to set up a sulfa drug assembly line staffed by natives of this world.

The trouble was, the process of production employed a number of toxic substances. As such, it was too dangerous to let anyone interact with them until they'd been properly educated on the hazards they posed.

Suppose Keine constantly supervised and instructed a group making the medicine. In that case, there likely shouldn't have been any issues. Still, given the amount of the compound that they needed to synthesize, it simply wasn't realistic to have Keine watch over the correspondingly high number of personnel that would be required.

"Gonna have Ringo make the medication, then? This is more her and Bearabbit's wheelhouse anyway, right?" Akatsuki asked.

"It is, and I imagine it would only take the two of them a few days to set up a production line. But as you know, Ringo currently has her hands full with *that other task*," replied Keine.

"Oh, right." At Keine's vague reminder, Akatsuki suddenly remembered the message he and all the other Prodigies had received. Tsukasa had contacted them all the night after he and Ringo had taken a day off together.

"Ringo's mission concerns the nation we intend to establish and is of the utmost importance. It can't be postponed, and I'd rather not add to her workload at the moment. We're only going to turn to her as an absolute last resort. First, I have someone else I'd like to test out. I wanted to see how useful her power might be to us going forward, so this will be an excellent opportunity to do so," Keine said.

"*Her power*" was the phrase that tipped Akatsuki off.

"Wait, do you mean...?"

Keine nodded. "That's right. I'm talking about Lyrule."

Behind the mansion that Keine was using as a hospital sat a courtyard. Placed in the middle of said courtyard was a massive, fifteen-foot-diameter cauldron. One after another, the medical staff carried blood- and pus-soaked bandages and clothes and tossed them into it.

Even in this world, it was an unusual sight. The reason for the unique ritual rested with the blond girl standing beside the large pot: Lyrule. Once the container had been filled with soiled dressings, she began to recite something.

"Water spirits…I call on you." As she murmured, Lyrule tapped her silver baton on the cauldron's rim. When she did, the water inside began swirling and swallowed the dirty things whole.

After about a minute of that—

"Ha!"

—Lyrule tapped the rim once more.

With a loud *poof*, a massive cloud of smoke billowed up from within. If one peered inside the cauldron after the curious little display, they would find that the bandages and clothes within were so clean they looked brand-new.

In effect, Lyrule was doing laundry.

Per a request from Keine, Lyrule spent her time with the medical team and handled all the group's laundry on her own.

"Wow, this is amazing! They're so clean and dry!"

"And the sheets are all fluffy!"

"This magic of yours is really handy, miss."

"Yeah, thank you! Clean bandages are worth their weight in gold for us. You're a lifesaver!"

"Oh, it was nothing. I wish I could do more to help."

There wasn't a single staff member who didn't thank Lyrule profusely as they retrieved the various pieces of clean cloth from the cauldron.

After a modest reply, Lyrule turned away and spoke her own words of gratitude to empty air.

"And thank you all."

Seeing that, a blue-robed man behind her spoke up.

"…You conversed with the spirits, didn't you?"

The man, Gale Stafford, was a former First-Class Imperial Mage and was currently working as Lyrule's magic tutor. Lyrule answered his question with a nod.

"Yes. All I did was ask them to remove the dirt and grime from the laundry. Really, the little spirits were the ones doing all the hard work."

Gale let out a small sigh of amazement. Listening to the spirits' voices and bending them to one's will was Magecraft 101. The interaction was fundamentally one-sided, however. Magic involved envisioning a spell and commanding the spirits to carry it out. In essence, that was how the process worked. Having a true back-and-forth conversation with spirits wasn't supposed to be possible. Even back in the imperial capital, Gale had never heard of a mage doing anything of the sort. As he saw it, Lyrule possessed extraordinary talent.

Even just finishing the laundry, a task Lyrule had achieved in a mere minute, would've taken five average mages a full hour to complete. What's more, such a task was sure to be incredibly draining, leaving those five mages completely useless for some time. To Gale's astonishment, however, not only had Lyrule finished her task in the span of a single minute, she didn't seem weakened in the slightest.

Lyrule's instructor still considered it something of a waste, however.

"If only you turned those talents of yours to battle. You would truly be a force to be reckoned with..."

As Gale sighed, Lyrule looked down apologetically.

"I know. I just...I can't envision telling these little ones to hurt people..."

Lyrule's gift for magic was incredible, but there was one type of magic she just couldn't get a handle on: offensive magic. Her gentle disposition made it difficult to hold an image of wounding others, let alone killing them. In that regard, her talents might as well have been nonexistent.

When it came to fighting, Lyrule would've had more success picking up rocks off the ground and throwing them at people. She was completely unfit to set foot on a battlefield.

Despondent over her inability to fight, Lyrule cursed herself.

"I'm terrible, I know. Everyone else is fighting so hard...while I..."

"Not at all" came a female voice that refuted Lyrule's self-deprecating words.

"Keine!" Lyrule exclaimed.

Akatsuki and Aoi accompanied the doctor making her way into the courtyard.

"Everyone has things they're suited for and things they aren't. War may not suit you, but that's hardly a problem. Besides, cleaning clothes and bandages for the wounded is a battle in and of itself. With over five hundred patients, managing their laundry is quite the ordeal. We're depending rather heavily on your ability to clean them instantly, you know. In fact, I daresay that without you, this hospital would barely even function. You're as far from terrible as they come."

"I'm...I'm glad to hear that." At Keine's earnest words of appreciation, Lyrule lifted her head and beamed warmly.

Keine responded to Lyrule's smile with one of her own, then quickly got down to business laying out the reason for her visit.

"...However, there's another task I need your help with today," Keine said after explaining the situation.

"Hmm? What kind of task?" asked Lyrule.

"You're going to prepare the medicine to save the patients suffering inside."

"I-I'm making medicine?!" When she heard what her new job was, Lyrule began panicking. "I—I can't! I don't know the first thing about restoratives..."

"I'm well aware, which is why I'll be instructing you every step of the way. We need your help, though. Your magic is essential if we're to synthesize the drugs."

"It is…?"

Keine nodded.

When viewed from an outside perspective, what exactly was the magic of this fantastical world? Of the High School Prodigies, Ringo, Tsukasa, and Keine had a shared theory on the matter. Specifically, they believed it to be a technique that allowed one to manipulate objects on an atomic level.

Creating fire from nothing, removing dirt from laundry, and extracting oils from rose petals were all possible via a manipulation of particles too small to be measured even with micrometers. If the Prodigies' mutual hypothesis was correct, then that power surely held untapped applications in all manner of fields. Keine's goal was to use her own knowledge to put those functions into practice.

"I'll be right next to you, giving you instructions the entire way, but we can't do this without your help."

"B-but…" Lyrule remained uncertain.

Everyone knew how dangerous it was for an amateur to try to make curatives.

Her tutor, Gale, gave the elf a little push.

"Go on, give it a try."

"But, Teacher…"

"Your skills are being wasted just handling laundry all the time. You must realize that on some level yourself, don't you? You're capable of greater things."

"But…that's…"

"Go make use of those talents of yours."

Lyrule hesitated for a moment, then turned to Keine.

"If I make this medicine…will it really help those people?"

"Yes, of course. It's the only thing that can."

Upon hearing that, Lyrule seemed to make up her mind. If her power could be used to help all those suffering in the hospital…

"…Okay. I'll do it. Or rather, please, let me help!"

Thus, the first-ever joint project between Earth's knowledge and this world's magic began.

Having secured Lyrule's assistance, the High School Prodigies took the chemicals Keine had gotten Ringo to send over from Dormundt, along with the massive iron "magic crucible" Lyrule had received from Gale to use in her training, and took them into the woods near the mansion. Attempting to create the necessary medicine inside risked exposing the patients to toxic chemicals.

After they'd set the crucible down on the ground, Keine began.

"Let me explain how we're going to make medicine out of coal tar."

"Y-yes, please," Lyrule replied.

"Now, the first thing we'll need to do is extract the component we want from the tar."

"We won't be using the coal tar as is?"

"No. Coal tar is a mixture of all sorts of things, but all we need for the medicine we're making is the benzene component from it. As such, our first mission is to isolate the benzene."

"But how do you do that…?"

"Normally, we would take advantage of the materials' different boiling points and utilize a process called fractional distillation. Benzene's boiling point of approximately eighty degrees Celsius is the lowest out of all coal tar components. To put it simply, you can think of it as the first thing that evaporates when coal tar is heated. However…" Keine paused for a moment to take a metal flask and pour a clear liquid from it into the iron cauldron. "…None of that will be necessary today. Ringo was using benzene as a raw material for something else, so she already had some on hand."

"Eww, this water smells oddly sweet…!" Lyrule scrunched up her face at the clear liquid's aroma.

Akatsuki took a whiff, too. It definitely smelled a little syrupy, but it wasn't a nice, fruity sweetness. It was a dangerous, chemical sort of scent.

All present but Keine had to wonder if Ringo really was using such a strange liquid to produce something.

"Hey, Keine, what exactly is Ringo using this stuff for?" Akatsuki asked.

"Bombs," she answered flatly.

""WHAAAAAT?!?!"" the others exclaimed.

"Bombs, I said."

"F-for real…?" inquired Akatsuki, as if fearful of hearing the answer.

"Yes. Benzene is used to make the infamous trinitrotoluene, better known simply as TNT. Gunpowder doesn't even come close to its destructive capabilities. Oh, and take care you don't breathe too much in. It can prove quite fatal."

"Fatal?! Oh dear… Ohhh dear…" Lyrule pulled away with a frightened look.

"K-Keine! You want us to dose the patients with explosives?!"

"Oh? Akatsuki, surely you know that scientists have used the famously explosive nitroglycerin as a heart medication, don't you?" Keine asked rhetorically.

"Oh, uh… Now that you mention it, that sounds familiar. I might have seen something about that in a TV show or an anime once…"

"Well, it's true. So as you can see, there's no rule that says bomb components can't be used in legitimate pharmaceutical products. I assure you, there's no cause for worry." Having made her case, Keine began describing how they were going to synthesize sulfa drugs.

"In any case, our process today begins with this benzene. Now, Lyrule, from here on out, I'm going to need you to follow my instructions to the letter. If you don't, it's liable to cause serious problems."

"L-like explosions?!" Lyrule shrieked.

"Quite possibly," Keine explained calmly.

"Eep..."

"But as long as you do exactly as I say, we'll all be fine."

"...G-got it."

Keine laid on the pressure with her smile, and Lyrule gave the doctor an ashen-faced nod. With the powers of magic and science working in unison, the sulfa drug production began.

The antibacterial properties in sulfa drugs came from a component called sulfanilamide. Isolating the benzene from coal tar was the first step in producing sulfa drugs. Adding sulfuric acid and nitric acid yielded nitrobenzene, which could be reduced to obtain aniline. From there, acetic acid was used to solidify the aniline into acetanilide. Finally, adding sulfuric acid and an ammonia solution would, after additional processing, yield the final product.

Lyrule carried out the steps under Keine's instruction, using magic to stir the liquid, regulate the temperature, and remove unneeded components in the form of steam. However...

"In this next step, we'll be using a chemical called sulfuric acid. However, there's something crucial I need to note first."

"What's that?"

"Touching it will kill you, so please make sure you refrain from doing so."

"Why is everything here so deadly?!"

"Hwa-wa-wa?! Keine, the water! The water in the cauldron turned into milk all of a sudden!"

"Not to worry. Liquids change color all the time, you know. Now, after a little bit, a substance resembling oil will float to the top. That's what we need, so when that happens, please use your magic to get rid of everything else."

"Now, we add this ammonia solution."

"That reeks…! Why does it smell like pee?!"

"Well, it's quite similar to highly concentrated urine. I should think it quite natural that it smells that way."

"Are you *sure* we're making medicine here?!"

"Don't worry."

"I'm a little worried!"

The process of synthesizing sulfanilamide wasn't difficult in and of itself, but hearing about the myriad toxic substances and seeing the color changes, crystallizations, and other chemical reactions sent Lyrule into a tizzy.

The elf had to wonder if it was truly safe to administer such a concoction to people, and her doubts only worsened by the minute. Even so, she made sure to carry out her instructions properly.

"Fire spirits, I call on you."

After a long series of steps, Lyrule used fire spirits to evaporate the last remaining undesirables from the crucible. All that remained was a fine white powder.

©Sacranec

Keine picked up a pinch of it, then abruptly gave it a lick.

She turned to Lyrule and smiled.

"…It's finished. Well done."

"Th-thank goodness…"

Upon hearing the good news, Lyrule breathed a deep sigh of relief.

"This powder is medicine?" Akatsuki asked.

"Yes. This sulfanilamide is the essence of sulfa drugs—the source of their antibacterial properties. Turning this into doses we can administer to people will take a little more work, but the active ingredient is complete. With this, we'll be able to save everyone from their sepsis."

"Huzzah! I shall go inform Elch and the doctors of this at once, that I shall!" Aoi exclaimed.

"Oh, I'll come along. If I order them to listen, it'll make the explanation go faster!"

With that, Akatsuki and Aoi headed back to the mansion.

Keine watched them go, then peered down into the crucible. By her estimation, the yield looked to be about three hundred grams. Given the amount of chemicals they'd used, it was admittedly on the low side. In all likelihood, the acid had melted the inside of the crucible a little, causing a number of unwanted reactions. The fact that they'd used concentrated sulfuric acid for the sulfonation instead of chlorosulfuric acid had probably also been a factor.

Such details were negligible for the time being; what was important was that the process had been extremely quick.

Notably, the spirits were able to classify components. The most time-intensive aspect of synthesizing compounds like that was refinement. The spirits allowed them to reduce that drastically.

With a container designed to be used with toxic substances, Keine thought it possible to produce pharmaceuticals with an impressive degree of efficiency.

…This is a far better way to use mages than deploying them on battlefields.

Thanks to Ringo, the Seven Luminaries could mass-produce firearms, meaning that battlefield mages weren't especially important to them. Keine made a mental note to propose to Tsukasa that they explore the medical applications of alchemy, the combination of magic and science, further.

Having completed the sulfa drugs with Lyrule's help, Keine processed them into injection doses and administered them to the patients in critical condition. Milinda, the girl from Coconono, was one of them, of course.

Day one: no change.

Day two: no change.

Day three: still no change.

Emelada's desperate pleas seemed to be falling on deaf ears. Milinda refused to wake. Her eyes remained closed, and she continued to writhe in agony. Her persistent lack of improvement cast a heavy gloom over the sickroom.

While no one said it aloud, everyone was wondering if it really had been impossible to make medicine out of coal tar. Even Lyrule, the one who'd actually synthesized the stuff, felt the same.

Worrying that she'd messed up Keine's instructions, her face grew paler by the day. By the third, she was as white as a sheet.

"Are you worried?" Keine asked with concern.

Lyrule bobbed her head up and down. "I mean…we were using all sorts of dangerous liquids that could melt your skin just by touching them, right? There were no medicinal herbs… We just made it from that black, goopy stuff... We even put in p-p-pee... I have to say, it's all a little scary."

Not a moment after Lyrule had finished, she realized that what she'd said could be taken as an insult to Keine and frantically apologized.

"I-I'm so sorry. As an amateur, I shouldn't doubt you."

Keine just smiled, not seeming to mind in the slightest.

"That's quite all right. At best, this world wouldn't have invented synthetic antibacterials for another five hundred years. Even then, you would have only stumbled on them after a long series of mistakes and failures."

Lyrule's reaction was entirely reasonable. What Keine had produced was a substance wholly alien to this world. It was only natural that a native had difficulty trusting its effects.

"But now, that history will never come to pass. Our actions have already irreparably altered your world's path. Going forward, you'll likely witness innumerable things you once thought impossible. At times they'll confuse you, worry you, and likely downright terrify you. Just know that all of this is for the sake of this world and its people. For now, I ask that you please put your faith in us."

Lyrule's response was quiet but firm nonetheless. "...Okay." She nodded. Truthfully, she still didn't understand what was going on or even what it was that she'd made. Despite that, Lyrule knew from first-hand experience that Keine and the rest of the Prodigies were worthy of her trust. That was why she chose to believe them.

Come the fourth day, a miracle happened.

"Ah... Ma...ma...?"

As Milinda's consciousness returned, she fixed her gaze firmly on her mother.

"Mi...linda? Milinda! You can recognize me?!"

The young girl replied to Emelada with a weak but definite nod. At last she had awoken again. Her consciousness wasn't the only thing that had returned, either.

"Her temperature and pulse rate have been stable since yesterday!"

"Inflammation is decreasing across her body! I can't believe she's recovered to such an extent already!"

""Fuck yeah!!!!""

Upon hearing the good news from the other doctors, Mash and Elch both threw a fist in the air and let fly cries of joy. Mash, however, immediately remembered how Keine was always going on about how, *"Giving the patients a sense of security is part of a doctor's job as well, so take care to avoid vulgar language."* A moment too late, he clamped his mouth shut.

"Erm, s-sorry...," he apologized, hoping it would keep Keine from getting mad at him.

She merely offered a smile in reply and raised her fist in the air with them.

"'Fuck yeah' indeed."

Milinda wasn't the only one feeling better. The door to the girl's room flew open, and several other doctors barged in. Each was out of breath and wore a joyful expression.

"Doctor! All the unconscious patients we gave sulfa drugs to are starting to wake up! The medicine is working!"

News of one recovery after another came streaming in. Lyrule, overjoyed and relieved, collapsed to the ground.

"Th-thank goodness... Thank—thank goodness..."

She knew Keine's drug would do the trick but had been terrified that she herself had bungled the preparation and so had fretted the past few days away thinking that the concoction wasn't going to work.

Perhaps because she'd sensed as much in the elf, Keine placed a hand on her shoulder. "You did well, Lyrule," she said, expressing heartfelt gratitude. Keine wore the same sort of unflappable smile she always did, though that was to be expected.

To her, the patients' recoveries weren't miracles or anything of the sort. Everything had been the natural result of the treatment she'd administered.

Consequently, the celebrations were going to have to be kept short. Keine understood all too well how much work there still was left to do. Clapping loudly to gather the staff's attention, Keine began to issue new instructions.

"Let's save the celebrating for when *all* of our patients are fully healed, shall we? We're expecting a shipment of penicillin from Dormundt this afternoon. When it comes in, we need to administer it to the patients, prioritizing those who showed allergies to sulfa drugs on the patch test. With our two-pronged attack of antibiotics and synthetic antibacterials, we'll cure this sepsis for good. It's about to get busy around here, so look alive."

""""Yes, ma'am!!!!""""

At their trusty leader's orders, the staff immediately got to work.

"Blessed angel!" Emelada rushed over to Keine, knelt before her, and bowed low. "Thank you! Thank you so much! I'll never forget what you've done for us!"

Keine refused the gesture, however. "Please, ma'am, lift your head. It wasn't me who saved your daughter. It was you."

"Me...?"

"Yes, you. The sulfa drugs we gave your daughter didn't have the power to kill the infection ravaging her body."

"Huh?! They didn't?!" Lyrule, the one who'd made the medicine in the first place, was the most surprised to hear Keine's admission. She'd been under the impression that what she'd created destroyed the infection.

"Penicillin has bactericide properties, but sulfa drugs… Well, to put it simply, they merely gag the bacteria in the blood and prevent it from eating more than it already has. They have the power to hamper the bacteria's activity and prevent it from multiplying, but they lack the ability to kill it. The human body, however, possesses that power as a natural function. It came from within the child herself. All I did was take your daughter's will to live and give it a little boost. The one who truly beat the infection was her. And when her suffering caused her to lose consciousness, the reason she never gave up on life…was because you were there by her side the whole time supporting her. This victory belongs to you two. Congratulations," Keine declared.

"Thank you…Mama… I heard your voice calling me…the whole time…"

"Oh, honey…!" Emelada's throat trembled. As her daughter smiled, Emelada wrapped her in a tight embrace.

In truth, the only reason such a dramatic recovery had been possible was because Keine used her needles to strengthen the girl's immune system to its limits. She certainly wasn't gauche enough to mention that part out loud, though.

With nothing left to do for Milinda, Keine turned her gaze from the mother and child to Aoi, Akatsuki, and Lyrule.

"Now then, we should go assist the rest of the staff. But first, the three of you need to go wash your teary faces."

"O-okay…"

"*Snf*, got it…"

"Aye!"

The three of them pitter-pattered out of the room and headed for the water well.

Keine herself was about to follow after when she noticed something.

…*Oh?*

Beyond a window, she spotted a man sitting atop a horse out of the corner of her eye. He wasn't a member of the medical staff, but Keine recognized him all the same. It was one of Count Selentius's lackeys.

His gaze wasn't trained on Keine but rather Lyrule, who was making her way out of the room. Even from a distance, Keine could make out the animosity in the man's eyes.

When Lyrule disappeared from the man's line of sight, he spurred his horse on and departed from the mansion grounds.

Keine smiled. "Hmm-hmm… Oh my. What a bad, bad boy he is."

Her grin was cold and chillingly beautiful.

That evening, the Healer Association doctor who'd gone and spied on the Seven Luminaries returned to his chairman, Count Selentius. He reported that the angels' curative had caused the patients to make dramatic recoveries.

The count went pale at the report.

"I-impossible…! You mean to tell me they really made medicine from coal?!"

"I'm not sure…but there's no mistaking that the ill did recover."

"What now, Count?! At this rate, they'll put us out of business for good!"

"Tch… You think I don't know that?!"

Count Selentius clutched at his head and moaned.

How utterly vexing it all was to him. Were it possible, he would've preferred it if that angel doctor simply up and disappeared. The Seven Luminaries were too powerful for that, however. Selentius knew that only a fool would openly pick a fight with a group like theirs. At the same time, if things were allowed to progress as they were, the Healer Association would shrivel up and die.

Th count ground his teeth as he racked his mind on what to do. Then—

"…Actually, I may have an idea."

—the man who'd gone scouting spoke up.

"What?"

"When I looked into how they were refining that red medicine, I found out that they're using that mage girl of theirs to make it. The angel seems to know *how* to make it, but she can't mass-produce it independently. That's why they need the mage. In other words…" The man broke into a grin. "…If we were to end her life, it might well stop them from making more."

"_____!"

The suggestion instantly replaced the count's anguished expression with one of glee.

"I love it…!"

Killing an angel was likely to be difficult. They seemed to possess strange powers and incredible knowledge. Assassinating a single mage, however, was child's play.

"But it would be a waste to kill her off, eh? We should…put her talents to better use."

"…Such as?"

"We could use her to sully the Seven Luminaries' reputation. After all, since she's the one making the medicine…couldn't she just as easily swap in poison?"

The count's lips curled into a sinister grin. Such a display of guile sent an excited stir through his lackeys.

"Splendid plan, Count!"

"Yeah! Once all their patients die, their influence will plummet! And when that happens, they won't be able to stop us from selling opium anymore! The only problem is, how to get the girl to help us…"

"Oh, please, a little girl like that? Once we kidnap and torture her a bit, she'll be eating out of the palms of our hands."

"How devious."

"Heh-heh, nice. I'm on board, Count."

With the approval of his toadies, Selentius rose from his couch.

"Then it's settled. I'll get in touch with our operatives at once and have them—"

Whatever the count had been planning to say was never heard, as the arrival of another had cut him off.

"Hmm-hmm-hmm. You know, I had a feeling you lot would come up with a plan like that."

"""_____?!?!"""""

This new, female voice sounded exasperated yet utterly calm. A few of the assembled members of the Healer's Association recognized it, too.

"Impossible," they muttered as they turned in unison to look toward the room's entrance.

At the doorway stood the doctor of the High School Prodigies.

"Good evening, everyone. Lovely moon out tonight. Wouldn't you agree, Count Selentius?"

"Keine...!"

"H-how did the angel find us here?! And what happened to our lookouts?"

"They were in the way, so I had them take a little nap. Like so."

Suddenly, Keine's white gown fluttered in the low light as she threw something with her right hand.

A pair of silver streaks, needles, flashed in the dark. The little things sped toward the two men stationed at either side of Count Selentius.

"Urk—"

"Ah..."

The little projectiles sank into the chests of their targets, and the pair promptly fell unconscious. They were special needles, designed initially to apply anesthetic to hard-to-reach places.

Bearing witness to an adolescent girl taking down adults in an instant, Selentius cowered in terror.

"Y-yeeeeeeeek!" he exclaimed. Face twitching all the while; the count tried desperately to plead with Keine. "Wh-wh-what do you think you're doing?! This is a gross violation of our agreement!!"

"Oh, there's no need to glare so angrily. I just want you to cooperate with us and abandon your plans to sell opium so the Seven Luminaries and the Blue Brigade continue getting along. That's why I'm here—to persuade you."

"D-don't be a fool! If you think there's still room for discussion after this, you're—"

Keine's eyes went wide, as if Selentius had said something surprising. A moment later, the doctor covered her mouth and let out an elegant little laugh. Perhaps the word *cackle* would've better described it, however.

"You misunderstand me. I have no intention of *discussing* anything with you."

As she spoke, Keine took a step forward, allowing more light from the hearth to be cast on her. It was only then that the count finally caught sight of what Keine had brought with her.

Clutched in her left hand...was a saw.

"—! Y-you mean to torture me...?!" Selentius's face lost all color.

"Perish the thought," Keine replied with a snicker. "I'm not a barbarian, you know. I'm a doctor. Weren't you listening? I came to *persuade* you...by tapping into your mind directly.

"Changing a man's mind with torture is simply *far too inefficient.*

"It's vastly preferable to meddle with his brain directly. Doing so can change not just his opinion, but his entire personality altogether. That way, he can be altered to become more…cooperative."

In short, torture paled before what Keine was proposing.

"E-eeeeeeeeeeeeeeeeeeek!!!!"

Hurriedly rising to his feet, the terrified man rushed toward a window. Despite his very best efforts, the count never reached his chosen avenue of escape. He'd collapsed onto the ground. Curiously, his left leg felt as heavy as a boulder.

"Agh! M-my leg!" he exclaimed, noticing a needle stuck in his left calf.

Keine had thrown it, striking a pressure point to paralyze his body.

Rather roughly, Keine lifted the immobilized count and turned him upright. Then she planted herself atop his chest, straddling him.

"Hold still now, please." After grabbing his hair to steady his head, Keine placed the saw blade against his temple.

The abject terror that overcame Selentius as he pictured what was about to happen to him sent tears, snot, and urine gushing from his body.

"F-fiiiine! You win! I give up! No more selling opium! We won't get in your way, and we won't lay a finger on your associates! I—I pledge eternal loyalty to you! I-I'll do whatever you say, just please, spare meeeeeeee!!!!"

For all his sobbing, Keine's smile didn't so much as waver.

"Really now, there's no need to be so frightened. The anesthesia will kick in soon."

"…!"

Suddenly, the count was overcome with drowsiness, though perhaps that was too romantic a word.

The sensation was closer to arms reaching up from the ebon and forcibly dragging the man's mind back down with them. It was a

©Sacranec

violent robbing of the senses that Count Selentius was powerless to resist.

He knew that his current self would be lost forever if he passed out, and some stranger would have replaced him when he woke back up. The count bit down on his lip so hard it drew blood, but it proved a fruitless bit of resistance. The man's vision darkened, and his consciousness grew dim. With the last of his energy, he spat one final epithet.

"Y-you're…a demon…"

Keine's reaction, however, defied all expectations.

"Ah-ha. Ah-ha-ha-ha-ha! How exquisite…!"

She smiled, and it wasn't the usual one she intentionally wore to set her patients at ease, either. It was an expression of heartfelt glee. Evidently, Keine was so elated that she couldn't keep it to herself.

"I much prefer that moniker over being called something as cold and aloof as an angel."

"—?!"

Blasphemy spilling from her mouth, the corners of Keine's lips stretched so high her cheeks seemed liable to rip. When the doctor drew her face so close to Selentius that he could practically feel her breath, he saw a deep hatred in her eyes.

Two pools of a deep, black loathing rested above Keine's nose, and the count could've sworn they were sucking him in.

"You'll forget all of this anyway, so let me confess a little something to you, Count. If an entity like a god truly existed, *I would despise it enough to kill it myself.*"

"…!"

"As a doctor, I've seen people suffering under countless ailments. Each time, I can't help but think that if God had built us properly and made our bodies and minds a little sturdier, humanity would never have had to suffer under the yoke of illness and war. It's utterly unforgivable if you ask me. What kind of incompetent creator builds such lovable creatures with such glaring flaws?

"I found myself compelled to swear an oath. *I vowed to take our inept creator's mistakes and fix them myself.* For those frail bodies doomed to die, I would grant eternal life. For those weak minds driven to harm others, I would impart perfect harmony. I swore to build a world where all would live forever, wanting for nothing. Yes…

"…I promised myself that I would become a god!"

"……——"

The young woman's hate-filled eyes gleamed with an unnatural light as she made her obsessive speech.

In that moment, Count Selentius realized that the girl before him was no angel, nor was she even a demon. Keine Kanzaki was something else altogether—a terrifying entity that could very well kill God someday.

While he desperately wanted to run and scream, the count's body was no longer capable of either. Eventually, his eyelids slumped shut—

"Now then, let's begin the operation to make you into a very good boy, shall we?"

—and the man named Selentius was cured of his malice.

Two weeks passed, and the first signs of spring began sprouting from the ground. A crowd of fully healed patients stood before the mansion.

With vigor in their strides, they hopped aboard one of the Seven Luminaries' trucks.

"Thank you for everything!"

"We'll never forget how much we owe you!"

"Long live the Seven Luminaries! Long live the angels!"

"And thank you, too, miss mage!"

The once deathly ill people waved good-bye to Keine, Lyrule, and the rest of the medical staff as cheers of joy and gratitude spilled from their mouths. The Bearabbit AI copy started up the truck and began the journey to deliver each of those cured back to their villages.

Lyrule watched the vehicle until it crested a hill; then she let out a long exhale. "Those were the last of the patients, right?"

"Yes, they were—the last of the ones being cared for at this camp, anyway. The fact we were able to send them off in good health is all thanks to you, Dr. Keine...and you, too, Lyrule," Mash said.

"O-oh, I wouldn't go that far. All I did was tell the spirits to do what Dr. Keine said."

"But only you could have pulled that off, right? I'd say that's still pretty darn impressive."

"Yeah, it is! You were awesome, Lyrule!"

"I—I..."

Hearing the medical staff heap praises on her made Lyrule squirm uncomfortably. She wasn't the type who enjoyed being lionized in the first place. From her perspective, she'd done nothing more than give the spirits instructions. The accomplishment hardly felt like it belonged to her.

Thankfully, Keine came to Lyrule's rescue.

"The two of us might have made the medicine, but what really brought them back to health was the diligent care you all gave them. Treat their smiles as a badge of honor. We also can't forget about the

Healer Association, who took on a large amount of the work part way through."

As if on cue, a man that the hospital staff all knew quite well came trotting over.

"Dr. Keine!" Count Selentius cried. Whatever animosity the man had once harbored had recently disappeared. In its place now lived a bright and cheerful expression. "Did you see those beaming faces of theirs?! Why, I've never felt so blessed to be a doctor before in my life! Patients' smiles truly are the best reward!" The man's eyes gleamed like those of an excited child, and his body practically radiated joy.

Keine nodded.

"I couldn't agree more. Thank you for all your hard work, Count. It looks like we're finished here for the time being. You should take some time off and let that head wound the burglar gave you heal up."

"Oh, I wouldn't dream of it! There's no time to spare, not with all the Gustav domain people who still need our help! The Healer Association is at your disposal, so please, just tell us what to do!"

"My, how eager. If you're sure, then after we finish prepping for teardown, we can talk about our next moves."

"I look forward to it!"

After giving an enthusiastic reply, Count Selentius took off at full speed. He hardly seemed to notice the blood dripping from the bandages wrapped around his own head.

Mash watched the curiously jubilant count make his departure with a dubious look on his face as he returned to the mansion.

"…I wonder what put old Count Selentius in such a cooperative mood. He said that he had a change of heart after robbers attacked his estate and left him for dead, but…it's more than his basic values; it's like he's a completely different person. It feels almost uncanny."

Mash wasn't the only one who'd noticed, either. Lyrule and the rest of the medical staff felt the same way.

One could've only wondered what had happened. Some thought it was a trick of some kind. Given the count's previous behavior, none of them could help but be suspicious.

Keine was quick to chide Mash, however.

"Now, now, don't say that. People change all the time, you know. Everything the man's done recently has been out of sincere regard for his patients. It's unfair to doubt him like that, don't you think? To the contrary, we ought to welcome our new ally with open arms."

"…You're right. If Selentius really were acting out of self-interest, he would never have handed over all the opium as he did. He must have taken a good, hard look at his past deeds and decided to turn over a new leaf. I guess I'm not really being fair to him. I'll try to be careful about that from now on."

Keine gave Mash's answer a satisfied smile.

"Good. Please do try to get along with him, everyone… After all, he's a very good boy now."

CHAPTER 4

❧ The Prerequisites of a Nation ❧

As the last of the snow melted, the smell of spring began permeating the land.

By and large, things were progressing precisely as Tsukasa Mikogami had expected.

Thanks to Akatsuki's magic shows and how proactive the Order of the Seven Luminaries was about providing charitable food and medical work, support for the group was slowly but surely rising among the Gustav domain's populace.

Health conditions in the domain had been questionable even in the best of times, so Keine's work, in particular, was the talk of the town. Many locals went so far as to pronounce the Seven Luminaries their saviors openly. On the other hand, the Blue Brigade's standing was plummeting.

While folks certainly gave them credit for rising to action and taking down Duke Gustav, that was all anyone attributed to them. They hadn't done anything of note since then, after all. The rebellious sect had been perfectly happy to dump all the cleanup on the Seven Luminaries.

That negligence stemmed from the fact that the Blue Brigade's leader, as well as many of the group's noble members, wished to spend as little of their own coin as possible. Such a tightfisted attitude was costing them quite a bit in terms of public favor, however.

When spring arrived, the Seven Luminaries had achieved a monopoly on the public's trust.

"The Blue Brigade is all talk."

"The Seven Luminaries care way more about us little guys than they ever did."

Gossiping housewives from villages all across the domain echoed the same sentiment.

As things worsened for his group, even Marquis Rommel von Conrad came to realize just how precarious a situation the Blue Brigade was in. If he allowed things to continue as they were, many were liable to start demanding the Seven Luminaries' installation as the new governing body.

Were such a thing to happen, Conrad knew the Blue Brigade wouldn't have the power to stand in their way. By slaying Gustav, the domain's imperially appointed duke, they'd earned the suspicion of their own country. They couldn't realistically expect help from the rest of the empire.

Standing on the edge of a proverbial precipice, Conrad had to wonder whether it was better to be assimilated into the Seven Luminaries. That decision would mean swearing to fight on behalf of the powerless masses.

Given the ideals Blumheart had founded the Blue Brigade under, it seemed the right thing to do, but Conrad couldn't accept that. As far as he was concerned, the very idea was laughable. Dividing up the privileges afforded to nobles and handing them to the common rabble was an idea so far removed from his way of thinking that it insulted his sensibilities to even consider it.

With that in mind, there remained only one other choice—Conrad had to get back in the empire's good graces as swiftly as possible. To that end, he penned a letter explaining the legitimacy of the decision to kill Gustav. He sent it off to Neuro ul Levias, one of the Four Grandmasters left in charge of maintaining order in the emperor's absence.

We imperial nobles fought for the sake of our great empire.

It didn't take long before Conrad's lobbying bore fruit. Soon, he and his titanic Gold Knight bodyguard, Zamuel du Reisenach, found themselves in Drachen, the imperial capital. They had been summoned to the audience chamber of the grandmaster's estate.

"W-will you really be enough to guard me on your own, Reisenach...?" The short, elderly Conrad fidgeted restlessly in the chamber's dim light. Rightly so, as the imperial capital wasn't exactly the safest place in the world for him.

If the empire had deemed the Blue Brigade's actions to be criminal, then Conrad had traipsed into the lion's den. Fully aware of that, the old nobleman remained ill at ease. His expression was dark with fretfulness and fear.

Conrad's gold armor-clad compatriot turned to him and replied, "If the empire really wanted us dead, we could've brought the whole Blue Brigade with us and it wouldn't have mattered. We want to demonstrate our lack of hostility, so coming without a full retinue of bodyguards gives off a better impression."

"Th-that's true, but it doesn't make me feel any better..."

"Our only option is to trust what the grandmaster wrote in his message, right?" As a glimmer of frustration crossed Reisenach's face at his master's cowardice, the two were greeted by a third voice.

"Oof. Sorry about the tardiness, gents. That war council meeting dragged on for aaaaages."

*   *   *

A jovial-sounding man sauntered into the room from the door opposite the one Conrad and Reisenach had entered from.

His hair was gray with a touch of blue, and his eyes were golden and gleaming. It was one of the Four Grandmasters who served Emperor Lindworm directly—Blue Grandmaster Neuro ul Levias.

"The Yamato survivors are taking advantage of His Grace's absence to scuttle around. To be honest, it's getting to be a bit of a headache. Ninjas have this obnoxious habit of popping up where you least expect them, see." Coolly explaining the reason for his delay, Neuro took a seat in the audience chamber's chair. "Anyhow, that's why I was late. Water under the bridge, I hope?" The man crossed his legs, his tone lighthearted.

Conrad lowered his already-short body and prostrated himself. "D-don't think twice of it! I understand how difficult it must be for a busy man such as yourself to find any time at all, honored Grandmaster. I thank you for being so gracious!"

"Ha-ha-ha. Loosen up, Conny. No need to be so formal. Don't tell me you're nervous, are you?"

"Sh-shamefully so, sir. I understand full well how tenuous my standing is."

Neuro cocked his head to the side.

"Well, that's odd. Didn't I send you a letter that said, *My greatest thanks to the Blue Brigade for deposing the fanatical traitor Gustav*, complete with my grandmaster seal? Well, no matter. Anyhoo, the empire views the Blue Brigade's actions favorably.

"We appreciate ol' Gus's devotion to His Grace, but come on. Moderation in all things. Starving the domain entrusted to him was out of the question. Besides, the survival of the fittest is the empire's national policy. Gustav was weak, so he became your prey, that's all.

"Your actions were fully in keeping with the spirit of the law, so they're to be commended, not reproached. We're not going to charge you with sedition or anything like that, so there's no need to look so spooked."

When Neuro restated his approval of the Blue Brigade's actions against Gustav, Conrad's face lit up with joy, and he bowed repeatedly.

"Th-thank you! As the Blue Brigade's representative, I extend to you our utmost gratitude for your understanding and—"

"There is one thing, however," Neuro cut in, his carefree tone suddenly turning grave.

Conrad's whole body broke out into a cold sweat as he waited for his superior to continue.

"…Those guys, see, they're trouble. What were they called, again? Right, right, the Seven Luminaries. They're a problem. Emperor Lindworm alone rules over the heavens and earth, yet they've been deceiving people with promises from a false god. That would be inexcusable enough on its own, but they've gone a step further and preached a message of equality for all. Such a stance flies in the face of the Freyjagard Empire itself. Leaving them to their devices simply isn't an option, now, is it? Ah, but I hear you've been getting pretty chummy with them."

"Th-that's, I…"

Narrowed golden eyes bored into Conrad, and he was struck by a wave of tension so powerful he thought for a moment that his heart had stopped.

Immediately, however, Neuro's expression gave way to laughter. "Ha-ha-ha, I joke, I joke." He seemed to be enjoying Conrad's timid reactions.

"Don't worry; I get it. I realize how delicate your situation is. I mean, we're talking about the powerhouses that took over three of the four northern domains in a single season here. The fight against Gus wore you down too much to pick a fight with them. I may not look it, but I'm one of the smarter Four Grandmasters. If anyone can appreciate your plight, it's me." Evidently, Neuro understood quite well the tricky predicament that Conrad had found himself in.

"Which is whyyy…I figured I'd offer you a hand."

Snap.

A sound echoed sonorously from Neuro's fingers. When it did, the door he came through opened once again, and another man made his appearance. This newcomer was hidden beneath a black overcoat and mask.

Between the man's unsettling appearance and aura, Gold Knight Reisenach's battle-honed instincts told him that the man was no mere eccentric. He leaned forward a bit as he spoke.

"Who is he? This man," inquired Conrad.

"My aide, Tanganika… Show them what you can do."

"———"

On Neuro's order, the masked man raised his bandage-wrapped right hand and held it up. In a flash, flame furled up in the audience chamber's fireplace, then whirled over to Tanganika's hand and began gathering atop it.

"Wh—?!"

"That's magic…! He's a mage?!"

The two of them goggled at the sudden supernatural phenomenon. Such a display was only the beginning, however. The flames gathered atop the man's hand started increasing in both heat and intensity, eventually transforming into pure red light. After only a moment, that glow had taken the shape of a spear in the mysterious man's hand.

Conrad and Reisenach recognized that red spear; anyone would've.

"Th-that's…!"

"W-without a doubt…that's Rage Soleil!!"

Indeed, the red spear was identical to Rage Soleil, the trump card of the man they'd fought against as members of the Blue Brigade.

It had taken Gustav years to finish one.

Yet, that man had conjured one in the blink of an eye.

"Tanganika is several times the mage Gus was. As you can see, he has the power to summon Rage Soleil in only a moment. Handy, right? And for now, I'm going to lend him to you."

"Wh—? R-really?!"

"Yup. And I'm dispatching soldiers to your location, too. Ten thousand of them."

"T-ten thousand?!"

"With that much might, you won't need to play nice with the upstarts anymore. Isn't that right?" Neuro gave a flash of his white teeth, grinning confidently.

Conrad shivered at just how assured the man seemed. He'd never know that the empire employed mages of such power. Truly, its power knew no limits.

The Freyjagard Empire is unbeatable…!

Conrad was coming to realize that allying his group with the empire was their only real option with each passing second. As such, he made his vow eagerly.

"O-of course! You have our deepest thanks for lending us a hand in our hour of need! With this, the Seven Luminaries will be powerless before us! We will eradicate those misguided fools who dare oppose the empire!"

"Ha-ha-ha. I should think so." Neuro chuckled, but then his gaze narrowed yet again. "With a grandmaster backing you to such an extent, I expect nothing less. Failure is not an option. Am I understood?" Unlike Neuro's joke from before, this time, the menace in his stare was real. Conrad felt it pierce his heart through.

His cheer from a moment ago gone, he went pale and prostrated himself yet again. "—! Y-y-yes!"

Neuro nodded in satisfaction. "That's what I like to hear... I leave squishing the pests to you, Tanganika."

Making those his final words, Neuro departed from the room.

After their meeting at the grandmaster's estate, Conrad and Reisenach stayed the night in Drachen. Then, the next day, they left the capital with Neuro's aide Tanganika in tow and headed for the Blue Brigade's Gustav domain headquarters—Fort Uranus.

"I never dreamed the meeting would go so smoothly... I'll say this, Grandmaster Neuro ul Levias is just as wise as the rumors claim. Between his ten thousand soldiers, our Blue Brigade, and your power, those commoners and Seven Luminaries stragglers are finished. They'll be dust beneath our boots in no time!"

"..."

During the carriage ride to the fort, Conrad tried to make small talk by expressing his gratitude toward Neuro as well as his admiration of Tanganika's magic, but the concealed mage was having none of it.

Well, aren't we a gloomy fellow?

Despite being complemented by an imperial noble—a marquis, at that—Tanganika wasn't offering so much as a single word of appreciation in return. Conrad thought there had to be limits to how rude a man could be.

Conrad made sure not to let his irritation show, however. Offending Tanganika wasn't an option. The mage was integral to the upcoming fight against the Seven Luminaries. After giving up on making conversation, Conrad headed to the back of the carriage.

Whispering in Reisenach's ear, he said, "When we get back to headquarters, I was thinking of giving our new friend an underground tour."

Reisenach, quick on the uptake, smiled. "You mean to give him some of the gold?"

"Exactly. In all honesty, the man unnerves me, but he has an in with the Four Grandmasters. That means he has a direct connection to the emperor. If we get him on our side and play our cards right, we'll be set for life. Whatever it takes, right?" Conrad replied gleefully.

"Heh. Nobody could stay that stony after getting an eyeful of that mountain of gold." Reisenach's grin broadened as he spoke.

Conrad and his allies within the Blue Brigade had stolen a veritable mountain of gold from Gustav and were keeping it for themselves. Just remembering the sight of it caused the old marquis's lips to curl.

However...

"...I wish I could agree, Reisenach, but *nobody* is perhaps a tad strong. Some hardheaded fools in this world refuse to see reason. Blumheart, for one. And to that point, there's something I need you to do before we settle things with the Seven Luminaries."

"Yeah? What's that?"

Conrad lowered his voice to make sure only Reisenach would make him out, then gave him the order. Upon hearing the hushed words, Reisenach's bandit-like visage curled into a barbaric smirk.

"Heh. You got it. Now *there's* a job that's right up my alley."

The Blue Brigade's headquarters, the massive and sturdy Fort Uranus, sat in the woods surrounding the checkpoint between the Gustav and imperial domains.

Ever since the empire's earliest days, Fort Uranus had stood as the emperor's shield. It had seen countless battles yet had never once been breached. Shinobu, who'd been left alone with the Blue Brigade, sat atop its rampart walkway. Her hair fluttered in the spring breeze as she gave Tsukasa her scheduled update.

Today, her report concerned the location of the gold statue she'd surreptitiously hunted down. It was also about the serious steps the Blue Brigade's leadership was taking to mend relations with the empire.

"Yup, basically. Looks like Marquis Conrad's made up his mind to return to the empire. He just went to a meeting in the imperial capital and only took a single Gold Knight with him. It'd take a real sweet answer to his initial letter to get a self-preserving coward like him to stroll into the capital."

"From the empire's perspective, it doesn't make sense to prosecute the Blue Brigade for sedition when they would much rather use them as a pawn against us. I expected as much."

"Anyhow, that about sums up stuff over here. What about you guys? How's Ringo's project comin' along?"

After Tsukasa's date with Ringo, he'd sent a message to all the other Prodigies informing them about a certain undertaking he'd requested of Ringo, one that was key to the founding of their new nation. Shinobu wanted to follow up on that.

Tsukasa's answer was prompt.

"She finished a few days ago. It's ready to use when needed."

"That's our girl Ringo. Reliable to a T."

"Thanks to Akatsuki and Keine's efforts, the Seven Luminaries have become very popular among the people of the Buchwald, Archride, and Gustav domains. All the pieces are in place to found our nation. Once we make the announcement, things will start moving fast."

"Sounds like I'm not gonna be here much longer, huh?"

"That's right. We know where the gold statue is, so there isn't much left for you to do there. Make sure you get out before things heat up."

"That's the plan. Conrad'll be back from Drachen soon, and I wanna hightail it before we bump heads."

"Then I'll see you in Millevana."

"Gotcha. Later."

Shinobu ended the call, then sighed. *Nothing left for me to do here, huh?* she thought. Tsukasa certainly hadn't been wrong. She'd dredged up all the intel there was to find, and now that the Blue Brigade was in bed with the empire, overstaying her welcome could easily prove fatal. Given that Shinobu made moves while others were prepping for the game, it was surprising she was still there at all. The ninja-journalist had her reasons, however.

"Ah, Ms. Shinobu!"

"Shinobu! It's been too long!"

A pair of cheerful female voices called out to Shinobu from behind. The girl turned to see the Silver Knight Jeanne and her *byuma* maid Elaine, who held a lantern. Shinobu had been waiting there specifically so she'd bump into the two of them when they made their rounds.

"True dat," Shinobu replied cheerfully.

"I hadn't seen you in a while, so I thought you'd gone back already," Jeanne said.

"Nah, I was just a teensy bit tied up. You on patrol?"

"That's right. Can't let anything happen while Marquis Conrad is away, after all."

"Look at you, bein' all diligent. Oh, hey, that reminds me. I got an update about that girl from Coconono you wanted to know about."

"You know what happened to her?!" Jeanne practically charged Shinobu.

"Hey, whoa there, girl," replied the startled ninja. She recited the news from the hospital exactly as Elch had told it to her. "Word is, she got discharged after making a full recovery."

Jeanne crumpled to her knees. "Is that so...? Oh, thank goodness... Truly..." Tears trickled down the woman's cheek as she breathed a deep sigh of relief.

On the day she and Shinobu had met in Coconono Village, Jeanne had given the order to have Milinda flogged. The girl's condition had been weighing heavily on Jeanne's mind ever since. A short while ago, Jeanne had asked Shinobu to pass along any news she heard about the poor girl.

As Shinobu saw it, Jeanne had made the right call to maintain her cover while the Blue Brigade was waiting to strike, but the heart and the mind were two separate beasts. Even though Jeanne knew why she'd had to do it, she lamented it all the same.

"Pardon me a moment."

With that, Jeanne drew the silver sword hanging from her waist. She held its blade straight in front of herself, then closed her eyes as though in prayer.

"_____"

A moderate amount of time passed before she opened them again, and Shinobu started to grow curious as to what Jeanne was actually doing.

"Were you praying?" the Prodigy asked.

Jeanne shook her head.

"No, not quite. I was just giving my report. Before the battle, my master was quite worried about the girl I'd had whipped, too..."

"Oh, now that you mention it, that's a different sword than the one you had back then. Is that..."

"Yes. It belonged to my master, Count Blumheart. It was presented to me after he passed. In addition to inheriting his family rank of count, he was also a Silver Knight himself."

"Sounds like you respected him a lot, huh."

"I wouldn't be who I am today if not for him."

Jeanne then recounted the story of her own origin.

Before she was a knight, Jeanne was just a common-born village girl. One day, the marquis who ruled over her village demanded her hand in marriage. She was only six at the time, while he was forty-eight.

The marquis had a reputation as a degenerate pedophile, and he well deserved it. Her parents, having heard the rumors, refused to hand Jeanne over. The moment they defied him, however, the marquis abandoned any pretense of civility. After having his soldiers cut down Jeanne's parents, he tried to rape her.

What had saved poor Jeanne had been a chance visit from Blumheart. He'd stopped in the village on a whim and came running when he heard the commotion. At the time, he was not yet a count and was known only as Granzham von Blumheart, Imperial Knight.

Blumheart dived into the fray and, in a marvelous display of swordsmanship, saved Jeanne by slicing off ten soldiers' heads, along with the marquis's penis. Doing so was not without repercussion, however.

As far as nobles were concerned, commoners were no different from livestock. The village was the marquis's to manage, so he was free to do with its people as he pleased. In short, Blumheart's intercession had been completely illegal.

To make matters worse, not only did the marquis hold a higher peerage rank than Blumheart's family's countship, but Blumheart hadn't even inherited the title yet. He was nothing more than a knight.

Although knights were permitted to call themselves nobles, they didn't have custodial rights over any land. As Dormundt's Zest once put it, they served a lord in exchange for coin, and at the end of the day, they were little more than glorified soldiers. A Platinum Knight, the highest rank a knight could achieve, was one thing, but anything below that was considered beneath even the status of a baron, the lowest rung on the peerage ladder.

The nobles came after Blumheart, demanding his execution. Yet, the knight refused to back down in the face of their tyranny.

Loudly, he proclaimed that overlooking such degeneracy sullied the empire's honor and that it was his duty as a knight to right such wrongs. Furthermore, he insisted that any member of the aristocracy who defended the marquis was just as much a deviant as the marquis himself and should be ashamed. As Blumheart openly antagonized the nobles, he also went around and formed a coalition of villagers and knights who agreed with him. In the end, they were able to shut the ruling class opposition up.

The knights who joined forces with Blumheart went on to become the founders of the Blue Brigade. The event also instilled Jeanne with great admiration for the man. Wanting to serve him, she begged her grandfather to let her enroll in the Knight Academy. In many ways, that event marked the beginnings of the Blue Brigade.

"Ever since that day, I continue to wonder how things might be if Count Blumheart had been emperor. What a beautiful country this might be were that only so," Jeanne concluded.

"You don't like the empire the way it is now?" Shinobu asked.

"No." Jeanne shook her head without a shred of hesitation or doubt. "Survival of the fittest might be a rule of nature, but if we just roll over and accept it, how are we any better than wild beasts?"

Jeanne thought back to the hideous mug of the man who'd tried to violate her as a child. In her eyes, that marquis was no human.

"People ought to strive to be nobler, more regal than that. Just as Count Blumheart was when he saved me back then. Just as you and your Seven Luminaries seem to be."

Jeanne firmly believed that people ought to help and support one another. Even if it brought no benefit to the one rendering aid, cooperation and living together harmoniously was best in her opinion. To

Jeanne, that was what separated humanity from the beasts. Blumheart may have died, but his protégé's convictions stood unshaken.

"Count Blumheart fell before he could see his ideals realized, but his will lives on in the Blue Brigade, and I intend to guard it with my life. I firmly believe that the day will come when those ideals will sprout and fundamentally change this empire for the better." With determination in her heart, Jeanne met Shinobu's eyes as she spoke. In the Silver Knight's gaze burned unyielding conviction—proof that the woman was far more than just talk.

Unfortunately, that was precisely what made Shinobu's heart ache so.

"………"

Shinobu knew that the Blue Brigade Jeanne was trying to protect didn't exist anymore. That was the reason Shinobu had stayed behind. With the way things were progressing, the Blue Brigade would soon be an enemy of the Seven Luminaries.

The group was to be made the empire's vanguard, and it would attack before long. Shinobu knew Jeanne's spirit was in the right place, however. By all rights, the Silver Knight should've been on the Seven Luminaries' side. They were the ones making Jeanne's ideals a reality, not the Blue Brigade. If nothing else, Shinobu wanted to get Jeanne into her camp before things got heated.

"Listen, Jeanne, you—?!" No sooner had Shinobu opened her mouth than her keen ninja senses picked up the lethal whizzing sound of something long and sharp.

"GET DOWN!"

Charging toward Jeanne and Elaine, Shinobu tackled the two other women to the ground.

"Ow! Ms. Shinobu, may I ask what you're— Huh?!"

Not a moment later, a massive barrage of crossbow quarrels

whistled past where the three had been standing. Arrowheads embedded themselves into the walkway wall.

"B-bolts?! Is it some kind of enemy raid?!"

"Not quite…"

Jeanne was only half right.

Thanks to Shinobu's exceptional night vision, she'd managed to spot the foe who stood on the other end of the passageway. Turning to face the assailant, she called to him.

"Shooting me makes sense, sure, but you wanna explain why you decided to go after Jeanne and Elaine, too, Gold Knight Reisenach?"

"Heh-heh. Fuckin' ninja. Even in the dark, you've got senses like a damn animal."

After having his identity revealed, Reisenach strode confidently out from the darkness. The man's presence seemed to baffle Jeanne.

"S-Sir Reisenach…?"

Why is a member of the Blue Brigade attacking us? Jeanne was at a loss, desperately trying to get a grasp on the situation.

Shinobu, on the other hand, understood the circumstances exactly.

"Looks like your meeting with the empire went well, huh?"

"Heh. Obnoxious bitch. How much do you know?"

"Oh, pretty much everything. I'm a prodigy journalist, I'll have you know."

"Dunno what a journawhatever is, but everything you've heard's probably true. The Blue Brigade is formally returning to the empire, so we have no use for you Seven Luminaries anymore."

When he spelled it out that clearly, even Jeanne could tell what was going on. The Blue Brigade had reconciled with its former master. In short, they and the Seven Luminaries were now enemies.

Indignant, Jeanne cried, "Reisenach, surely you know how much they've helped us! Can't you see what the Seven Luminaries have done for the Blue Brigade and the people of Gustav?! Returning to the empire and turning against them is one thing, but launching a surprise attack against our benefactors like that is the lowest of the low! Have you no pride as a knight?!"

Reisenach seemed quite amused by the plea.

"Heh-heh, ah-ha-ha-ha! Not in the least! Y'know, when your boss Blumheart died, he asked me the same damn thing. 'Have you no pride as a knight?' Like master, like follower, I tell you what. Bwa-ha-ha-ha!"

"When he died...? What do you mean by that?!"

There was an ominous quality to Reisenach's words. When Jeanne pressed him for clarification, he gave her a disparaging sneer.

"You're a couple of cards short of a deck, ain'tcha? I'm sayin' that the old fool died at my hands—the hands of Zamuel du Reisenach!"

"_____?!?!"

"Ha-ha. Please, don't act so surprised. Did you not see this coming? Look, Gustav was an asshole. You can screw with the rabble all you like, but when you start killing 'em off, it starts messing with *our* lives. But that doesn't mean all the Blue Brigade knights and nobles agreed with Blumheart's bullshit philosophy. I mean, c'mon. Why should we have to shed our blood, sweat, and tears for a bunch of worthless common trash?!"

The barbaric Gold Knight then revealed that other than the Blue Brigade's founding members, everyone else had been ready to push all the blame on Blumheart if they were ever exposed. Such was the truth of the group's corruption.

"But there's no need to keep a scapegoat around anymore once you win. Blumheart was just gonna get in our way. So we got rid of him. Heh, you shoulda seen the look on that dumbass's face. His big victory was right there in front of him, and boom, sword through the back. That shit was priceless!"

The truth of Count Blumheart's death had at last been revealed. His own allies had struck him down. Jeanne's crimson hair bristled up like a raging fire.

"YOU BASTAAAAAAAAARD!!!!"

The moment before the incensed woman could charge Reisenach, however, a dozen soldiers fanned out around him, barring the way forward.

Whirling around, Jeanne saw another group of fighters had appeared at the opposite end of the rampart pathway. She, Shinobu, and Elaine were trapped.

His position now unassailable, Reisenach began to boast of his plans again.

"Now that we have an Imperial Grandmaster on our side, we don't even need the Blue Brigade anymore. So we're crushing it—along with any idiots who idolize Blumheart and can't tell the difference between dreams and reality!"

It was a political purge.

Before they'd joined up with the empire, Conrad and the other nobles allied with him intended to wipe out all the Blue Brigade members who remained true to its founding ideals.

It's already started, huh? Shinobu had hoped to be able to get Jeanne out of there before that began, but clearly, it was much too late for that. The Brigade's meeting with the empire had gone far better than the Prodigy had anticipated. Perhaps this meant that Grandmaster Neuro was going to be more of a problem than Shinobu had first suspected. The girl gritted her teeth as she thought of their true, still-distant enemy.

"Jeanne, run! There's no way we can take on this many while protecting Elaine!" Shinobu insisted.

Jeanne refused to budge.

"...Shinobu. Take Elaine and flee."

"Mistress?!"

"That man killed my master. On my pride as a knight, I refuse to turn my back on him!" Without turning around, Jeanne pointed her sword straight at Reisenach. The air exuding from the woman expressed her convictions far better than words ever could have. Trying to persuade her was a pointless endeavor.

Shinobu, realizing that, called out, "Got it!"

"M-Mistress!" Elaine resisted, but Shinobu scooped her up by force, cradled her under her arms, and planted her foot on the edge of the ramparts in an attempt to leap off.

Reisenach's people were equally quick to react, though.

"Don't let them get away! Shoot 'em down!"

A volley of bolts lanced into the dark, however—

"HYAAAAH!!!!"

—not a single one reached Shinobu or Elaine.

Jeanne had immediately wrenched her cloak free from her armor and then used it for batting them all down. Taking advantage of the opening, Shinobu leaped off the ramparts with Elaine in tow and vanished into the forest below. Knowing Shinobu, there was no doubt she'd make a safe landing somehow.

"Tch! How's a woman like her so clever...?!"

Jeanne's quick thinking earned a grumble from the soldiers. Reisenach quickly reassured them, nonetheless.

"Doesn't matter. Once the empire's reinforcements get here, they're both dead anyway. Still, though..." The man's gaze shifted to Jeanne, and his expression filled with scorn. "...You really are a stupid little girl, aren't you? Shoulda gone with 'em. What do you think you can do on your own against these numbers? You think you're the protagonist of some fairy tale?"

"Shut up, scum. You and I have nothing to talk about!" Jeanne declared defiantly.

"Heh. Big words for someone in your spot. I like it. As an Imperial Gold Knight, I gotta respect that panache." With that, Reisenach donned his helmet; then he grabbed the cudgel that took three of his men to carry and hoisted it with ease. "One-on-one, me an' her. Nobody else interfere."

With stern obedience, the others heeded the order and backed off a bit. Jeanne's obstacles now gone, her revenge-fueled fury only seemed to burn brighter.

"You'll pay for what you did!!"

"Then make me!"

Reisenach made the first move. He dashed at Jeanne with a speed that seemed unthinkable for a man of his stature. Jeanne responded by taking her free left hand, grabbing the metal whip hanging from her waist, and cracking it.

"Hyah!"

The lash sped forward, covering a distance of over fifteen feet as it sliced through the air. Without a shield, Reisenach was powerless to block the attack.

"Ha-ha! This shit's light! So light I can barely feel it! You think you can kill someone with an attack like that?!"

Unfortunately for Jeanne, it did little to slow Reisenach's approach. Perhaps that was to be expected, however. Every inch of the man's massive body was covered in golden plate armor. With a layer of chain mail beneath to guard Reisenach's exposed joints, the man seemed an impregnable fortress. Only he, with his nigh-superhuman strength, could've worn protection like that. It repelled each of Jeanne's attacks—and eventually, he reached cudgel range.

"An attack, see…is supposed to be like THIS! HRAAAAGH!!" Reisenach brought his weapon down on Jeanne's head with all his might. He made no effort to bluff or feint—just one, big, brute-force swing.

Jeanne dodged backward, but…

"Ah…!"

"HRAAAAAAGH!!!!"

The spot where Jeanne had been standing on the stone walkway was shattered into pieces. Just dodging an attack like that wasn't enough. The shock wave from the impact dulled Jeanne's follow-up, and Reisenach took full advantage of that.

"You powerless! Feeble! WEAKLIIIIING!!!!"

"Rgh—"

The cudgel came crashing down again and again as though it didn't weigh a thing. Reisenach's skills were the real deal. Before she knew it, Jeanne found herself backed up against the soldiers behind her. Retreating any farther would've surely meant she'd find a sword in her stomach.

"Ha-ha! Now you've got nowhere to run. What're you gonna do now? What're you gonna do now?!"

"Don't make light of my whip!"

Jeanne was not without her own strengths, however. The woman hadn't risen to the rank of Silver Knight for nothing. Again, Jeanne launched her lash at Reisenach, this time aiming for the man's helmet. The piece's only openings were its small eye holes. Aiming for such a miniscule target was a fool's errand, which was precisely why that wasn't what Jeanne was trying to do.

"Wh-WHAT?!"

With deft manipulation of her whip, Jeanne twined the thing around Reisenach's headpiece, blinding him. Robbed of sight, Reisenach swung his club with large, wide sweeps. The aimless attacks gave Jeanne the opportunity to move in.

Tossing the handle of her whip aside, the woman pulled forth a short, thin sword from its place at her hip. It was a weapon designed for piercing chain mail.

"It's over—!" Jeanne cried as she charged.

However—

"Men! Fill this bitch with bolts!"

"—?!"

—the next moment, something unthinkable came from Reisenach's mouth, and a hail of quarrels bore down on Jeanne. With a hurried recklessness, the woman threw herself to the side. Fortunately, she succeeded in dodging the crossbow shots.

"HYUH!!!!"

"Agh!"

Less fortunate was that Reisenach used the opportunity to rip the whip from his eyes, restore his vision, and land a kick in Jeanne's side so hard it sent her tumbling across the walkway. As soon as she fell to the ground, the soldiers rushed at her and pinned her down from above.

"Geh... Reisenach, you lowlife! How low can you sink...?!"

The great bear of a man had sullied their duel, and Jeanne was furious.

"Shut up, you little shit! Your cheeky display back there made a fool of me!" Unreasonable as it may have been, Reisenach seemed just as indignant. "Death is too good for her! C'mon, men! Have your way with this bitch! Make her regret being born a woman!"

"...!"

"W-wait, we can?!"

"Nice! Y'know, I was just thinkin' how it'd be a shame to carve up a woman as easy on the eyes as her."

Vulgar smiles spread across the soldiers' faces, and they

immediately got to work stripping off Jeanne's armor. She tried desperately to resist, but their numbers were too much for her, and in a flash, the woman found herself defenseless.

"Get back! Stop it, you brutes! No, nooooo!"

"Hee-hee. Lady knights look so much nicer without all that armor."

"That smooth skin…don't mind if I do."

"——!"

Pinned as she was, the memory of Jeanne's childhood trauma surfaced in her mind, and tears rolled down her face.

Their carnal lust now ignited, the men didn't stop.

"C'mon, girlie, purr real nice for me."

"Eek—"

One of them tried to steal Jeanne's lips. Horrified at the prospect of having her first kiss snatched away like that, Jeanne decided to end things herself. The moment before she could bite off her own tongue, however, there came a most unexpected interruption.

"Gwaaaah?!"

A spray of fresh blood soaked her face.

Jeanne hadn't bitten through her tongue in a bid for suicide yet, so she had to wonder what'd happened. The explanation lay right before her eyes. The man who'd tried to kiss her had a black knife blooming from the inside of his mouth. Immediately, Jeanne recognized its shape.

That's a kunai! It can't be!

"Shinobu?!"

The moment she called the name—

""""AAAAAAAARGH!!!!""""

—the men pinning her down all collapsed, blood gushing from their necks.

"Looks like I made it in the nick of time, huh?"

A girl was standing before Jeanne with an oversized scarf wrapped around her neck.

It was Shinobu Sarutobi, prodigy journalist.

When Jeanne saw her savior, it didn't fill her with joy.

If anything, what she felt was anguish, not relief.

Jeanne was no expert on politics, but it didn't take a genius to realize where the Blue Brigade and the Seven Luminaries stood regarding each other. Shinobu was in enemy territory. Her refusal to flee put her in extreme danger.

"Shinobu...why did you come back?! These people are—"

Shinobu understood all of that already. The answer to why she'd come back was simple enough.

"'Cause leaving a friend behind is outta the question."

"...!"

When Jeanne heard Shinobu's answer...it sent a little pang of joy through her heart. She realized there was nothing more for her to say.

"Don't worry. I stashed little Elaine somewhere they'll never find her. Now, c'mon, get up. You still gotta avenge your master, right?"

Shinobu hadn't come back to get Jeanne to safety. She'd returned to ensure Jeanne saw her wish fulfilled.

"...You have my thanks!" With her opponent having already broken the duel, Jeanne had no reason to turn down Shinobu's assistance. The two of them stood back-to-back with their weapons at the ready.

Furious, Reisenach bellowed, "Quit standing around, you dolts! What's one more bitch to crush?!"

"""Y-yeaaaaaaaaaah!!!!"""

©Sacraneco

The soldiers obeyed the command, drawing their swords and charging. However, what they failed to account for was that their foes were the duo who'd stood together at the forefront of the battle with Gustav.

"Jeanne, *cover your eyes!*"

"Roger that!"

After giving Jeanne the signal, Shinobu threw a ninja flash grenade at their feet. It broke on impact, releasing a violent and luminous burst that instantly blinded the soldiers.

"Aaaagh!"

"I can't see any— Urk!"

With the soldiers sightless and flustered, the two women routed them in no time. A numbers advantage was meaningless if your forces couldn't see. Compared to Gustav, the soldiers were a cakewalk.

"Th-they're too strong!"

"Yeah, they're crazy strong!"

"Cowards, the lot of you…! Out of my way!"

""""Aaaagh!!!!"""""

Fed up with the incompetence of his underlings, Reisenach made his move. Sweeping his men aside with his cudgel, the Gold Knight strode forward.

"I'll crush 'em both myself!" With a mighty force behind it, Reisenach brought his great club down at Shinobu.

The ninja-journalist handily evaded the lethal attack, however. In the same motion, she moved right up to Reisenach and pressed her stun gun against his armor.

"Hzzzzzt?!"

Electricity flowed through Reisenach's plate and all across his body. The man convulsed violently.

"Jeanne! Now!"

Kicking off Shinobu's back and shoulder, Jeanne launched herself into the air. Soaring up such that her sword was level with Reisenach's head—

"I'm grateful you're wearing that fancy helmet of yours because your face is the last thing I want to see!"

—she thrust her stiletto through an earhole, skewering his brain from the side.

"Gluh—"

The attack punctured the cerebellum, and the giant man was struck dead instantly. His massive body toppled to the ground.

Two Imperial Knights had entered the duel, but only Jeanne du Leblanc left it.

"Wh—? Th-they killed Sir R-Reisenach!"

"Quick, go get reinforcements! We'll crush them with sheer numbers!"

While the soldiers were clearly frightened from what'd happened, they showed no signs of retreating. The order for the surprise attack had come from someone higher in rank than Reisenach, after all. If Shinobu and Jeanne remained for much longer, it was likely they'd find themselves quickly overrun.

"You got your payback, so let's not overstay our welcome. It's time to run for real, Jeanne."

"Understood!"

After calling out to Jeanne, Shinobu threw another bomb at their feet. No light was issued from it this time, though. Instead, a thick smoke billowed from the little thing.

"Wh-what's with this gas?!"

"It might be poison! Don't breathe any in!"

The Blue Brigade men all covered their mouths. That hesitance turned out to be their undoing, however, as when the smoke cleared, the two women were nowhere to be found.

"Th-they're gone! Where'd they go?!"

"Dammit, it's one weird technique after another with those two…! Find them! Whatever it takes!"

Frantically, the men scoured the fortress for their two missing foes but turned up nothing. There was no way they could've. Shinobu had picked a hiding spot *no normal soldier would've ever thought to check*, after all.

"Waaaaaah! Miiiiistresssss! Thank the heavens, you're safe!"

"Ow! No hugging, please, I have some broken ribs…"

"WAAAAAAAAAH!"

"Agh! Sh-Shinobu, some help here…!"

"Hey, just think of it as your punishment for going and doing something so dangerous."

The few torches hanging from the wall were the only thing illuminating the damp hallway. Elaine, Jeanne's maid, had hidden in the place per Shinobu's instructions. Upon being reunited with her master, Elaine immediately wrapped Jeanne in a teary embrace. Unsettling cracking noises echoed from Jeanne's body as she did.

Jeanne begged Shinobu to save her, but Shinobu was just as upset at the knight's recklessness as Elaine was, so she left Jeanne to her screaming until Elaine finally settled down and released her.

"Owww… Still, I had no idea this space existed beneath Uranus." Finally free, Jeanne had her first real chance to marvel at her surroundings.

The three were in one of the passageways that led through Uranus's underground basement. Apparently, Shinobu had discovered the tunnel only a day before.

"Not many know about this secret area. The normal soldiers have no clue it's down here, and the people who *do* know would never suspect I found it. It's the perfect spot for us to hide…or for them to hide something from us."

"Such as…?"

Shinobu's words were heavy with intentional implication, and Jeanne picked up on it immediately. Now that the Blue Brigade was being openly hostile, there was no need to keep it from Jeanne anymore.

"This way."

Shinobu led Jeanne and Elaine down the passageway to where the Blue Brigade's dark secret slept. Eventually, they reached a large, sanctuary-like area. Shimmering in the light of its surrounding braziers was a towering mountain of gold.

Utterly shocked, Jeanne's eyes went wide. "Th-that…that gold—that isn't…?!"

"'Fraid so. That's the statue of the emperor that Marquis Conrad claimed got sent to the imperial capital. The marquis and his friends smashed it to pieces and stashed it away. After they broke it down to keep it from being recognized, they were slowly selling it off and keeping the profits for themselves."

"How awful…"

"That statue was made with the people's tax money. No, that's putting it too lightly. It was sculpted by shaving the flesh from their bones! How could anyone try to line their pockets with that blood-stained metal?! Those shameless fiends!"

Elaine and Jeanne were aghast at the greed of it all. Shinobu found the debased act only a matter of course, however.

"That's just the kind of assholes they are. I mean, this is the group that murdered its leader and pretended he died in battle we're talkin' about here."

It was then, at last, that Shinobu was able to finish what she'd tried to tell Jeanne before they'd been attacked.

"Jeanne, I'm sorry, but the Blue Brigade's lost sight of the passion and ideals it started with. There's nothing worth protecting here anymore. Hasn't been since they killed Count Blumheart."

"..." Jeanne frowned, and her expression contorted in anguish. The Blue Brigade was precious to her. It was all she had left of the master she revered so strongly. Admitting that the group had lost its way was difficult. Between the surprise attack from before and the hill of gold before her eyes, however, that fact seemed indisputable. The woman's heart felt like it was going to split in two.

"That doesn't mean Count Blumheart's ideals are dead, y'know."

"Huh?"

"They live on inside of you."

"...!"

"You inherited that kindness, that sincerity, from him. None of that's faded, has it? A broken container's nothin' to worry about as long as its contents are fine. If the Blue Brigade won't accept what you and the count fought for, then we Seven Luminaries would be more than happy to have you.

"Come with me, and we'll change this empire together. We'll make it into a place where people can live with dignity."

With her gaze firmly fixed on Jeanne's red eyes, Shinobu offered the knight a handshake. Together, they would destroy the status quo. For Jeanne, making that choice would entail abandoning her home, the empire, and the Blue Brigade. It was by no means an easy decision.

"...If I'm being honest, I noticed the changes. Watching us shove all the restoration efforts onto the Seven Luminaries' lap while not lifting a finger ourselves never sat right with me. But...the Blue Brigade was everything to me, so I must have unconsciously avoided thinking about it too hard."

Jeanne knew it was just as Shinobu had laid it out. The Blue Brigade was nothing but a vessel. The Silver Knight ran her fingers across the sword hanging at her waist. Everything Jeanne held dear—Blumheart's ideals, his conviction, his will… All of them were right there. That being the case, there was no cause to falter.

"I suppose the time has finally come. For the sake of the will of my master, which lives on in this blade, and for my own sake as well, I will happily join you and yours."

Shinobu replied with a broad smile and a big, "Yay!"

Open war would soon erupt between the Blue Brigade and the Seven Luminaries. When that happened, the one thing Shinobu absolutely wanted to avoid was having to fight Jeanne. As the Prodigy rejoiced, Jeanne posed another question.

"Uranus aside, there are still worthy people in the Blue Brigade. Are those venerable men and women welcome as well? If I was attacked, it stands to reason that they might be in danger, too."

Shinobu answered with a big nod. There was no reason to refuse, after all.

"Of course! The more the merrier!"

"You have my thanks. As soon as we've escaped, I'll go to them directly and—"

"Hold that thought!" Shinobu exclaimed, cutting the other woman off. Thanks to her exceptional hearing, she'd picked up the sound of footsteps coming their way. The footsteps were as quiet as the sound of a faucet dripping another building over, but Shinobu heard them as clear as day.

"Someone's coming—hide!" Shinobu grabbed Jeanne and Elaine and dragged them both into cover.

No sooner had she done so than a massive door into the room loudly swung open. Two people entered.

That's Marquis Conrad… And the other one is…

Shinobu turned her gaze to Conrad's companion.

It was a creepy, masked figure concealed behind a large overcoat.

...Wait, huh?

As a prodigy journalist who'd made a life of interpersonal interaction, Shinobu had developed a kind of sixth sense. As soon as she laid eyes on that mysterious garbed figure, that sense went off. While she couldn't see the person's face, and the contours of their body were obscured, there was a vibe the strange character exuded that matched a certain individual exactly. That realization made Shinobu shudder.

Could it really be him...?

Over on the other side of the room, Conrad gestured to the large pile of gold.

"Well? A sight so splendid it dazzles the eyes, is it not?"

Not realizing that Shinobu and the others were present in the secret underground basement with them, Conrad showed Tanganika the stolen stuff.

"Those Seven Luminaries brats may call themselves angels and gods, but they're nothing more than gullible fools. I simply pretended to have lost track of the gold statue, and without questioning it, they agreed to pay for the relief efforts themselves. Suckers, the lot of them. Thanks to them, we got to keep all the treasures that Gustav hoarded for ourselves, this gold statue chief among them."

"You dismantled the statue?"

"...!"

That question marked the first time Conrad had heard the man speak since Neuro first bequeathed the odd mage to him. Amused, Conrad chuckled to himself at the change.

Seeing the gold must have piqued his interest and loosened his tongue. Excellent.

"Naturally. No trading company in the world could liquidate a sixteen-foot gold statue all at once, and the fact that it was shaped like the emperor would have been awkward for all parties involved. For instance, when the time came to share the wealth with a new friend, hmm?"

Conrad smirked as he took a softball-sized lump from the pile.

"Please, consider this a token of a long and fruitful friendship to come."

After placing it atop Tanganika's palm, Conrad took the other man's hand and the gold held in it, clasped them in his own hands—

"And, fortune willing, I hope for that friendship to extend to your lord, the grandmaster, as well."

—and made a roundabout allusion to his true goal.

Simply put, Conrad wanted Tanganika to help him make a good impression with Grandmaster Neuro.

"If that were to happen, you could expect ten times this amount to find its way into your pockets."

It was a rather blatant bribe on Conrad's part. In the empire, that sort of collusive relationship was all too common. Many a political war was fought behind closed doors.

The coward's ploy quickly ended in failure, however.

"I see… You really broke it…"

For the masked man, Tanganika, was not the sort who could be so easily enticed.

"Lord Tanganika? Agh—?!"

Suddenly, the mage lashed out with his bandaged hand, grabbing Conrad by the collar and hoisting the little man into the air.

"L-Lord Tanganika...what are you...?" Conrad's eyes darted about at his guest's sudden display of violence.

Tanganika spoke, his voice quivering with rage. "Rommel... Rommel von Conrad... Betray *me* all you like. Our emperor desires a world where only the fittest survive. I cannot fault you for that. But to take a hammer to a likeness of His Grace and destroy it...? You WRETCH!"

"...I-it can't be...!"

Hearing that voice speak such words, Conrad came to the same realization as Shinobu. For him, though, it came far too late.

"KNOW YOUR PLACE, CURRRRRRRR!!!!"

As Tanganika bellowed loud enough to send a slight vibration through the air, a flash of red flame burst forth from his body. The force of it shredded his overcoat and shattered his mask to pieces. His identity revealed, the man known as Tanganika was unmistakably...

"D-Duke Gustav?!?!"

It was indeed none other than the Fastidious Duke, Oslo el Gustav. A man who was supposed to have killed himself in the battle against the Blue Brigade was seemingly very much alive.

Conrad trembled, his face pale as a sheet.

"I-impossible! Y-you're supposed to be dead...!"

"You think I! Oslo el Gustav! Would die while vermin yet fester in His Grace's garden?! Don't you dare make light of my devotion! I may have been on death's door, but Lord Neuro's mystic arts brought me back from the pits of hell! AND I BROUGHT ITS HELLFIRE BACK WITH ME!!!!"

As Gustav screamed, the bandages wrapped around the arm lifting Conrad into the air steadily burned away. Flames coiled up and began swallowing Conrad whole.

"GYAAAAAAAAAAH!!!!"

It wasn't long before the older man's body was completely ablaze. Gustav hurled him down to the ground, and Conrad writhed about in agony as his flesh burned.

"Ah, it's hot—it burns, gah, AAAAAAARGH!"

Though Conrad rolled about on the stone floor, trying desperately to extinguish the flames, they refused to go out. Conrad's clothes burned, and his skin turned to ash.

"It…won't…go out… Reduced…to ash…but the fire…the fiiiiiiire…"

Conrad burned and burned, but the afterlife was a luxury not permitted to him. Gustav refused to allow it.

"Death is too good for traitorous scum like you. You will suffer for all eternity as my undead flame soldier."

Conrad writhed like a dying caterpillar as Gustav made his chilling proclamation. Everything about what she was seeing sent a shudder down Shinobu's spine. As if Gustav surviving and now torturing a traitor wasn't bad enough, there was something strange about the Fastidious Duke's aura. Shinobu had gone toe-to-toe with the man, so she could tell.

It was like he was a different man altogether. While he'd always been intimidating and carried a domineering presence, both of those features seemed heightened compared to the person Gustav was before. Shinobu made her living studying others, so it didn't take her long to deduce the source.

It's that thing… Gotta be.

Gustav's overcoat and tunic had been blown away, exposing his bare chest. Protruding from where his heart would've been was a pulsating black gem. Whatever it was clearly wasn't natural. Gustav had destroyed his shirt and bared his chest during Shinobu and Jeanne's battle with him, and he hadn't had anything like it back then. That could only mean it was something he'd acquired after his disappearance.

Shinobu didn't exactly understand the strange stone's purpose, but there was little time to consider it anyhow.

"Now then, I have a debt to repay…to you rats!"

Gustav's malevolent, bloodshot eyes swiveled toward where Shinobu and the others were hiding.

Crap!

Flames began to gush from the duke's body like a tidal wave and surged toward the three women. Shinobu had been considering a few angles from which to attack. However, that plan had to be tossed out the window. It was very clearly time to leave.

"Jeanne, run!"

They'd beaten Gustav before, but that unnatural strength he was emanating told Shinobu that going for a rematch would be a bad idea.

Jeanne appeared to share the sentiment.

"R-right! Elaine, with me!"

"O-okay!"

The three of them turned and fled. They headed back the way they'd come, trying desperately to escape the burning wave at their heels. The scorching tongues of flame refused to allow such an egress, however, forming burning hands to grasp at the trio. Hundreds of burning arms twisted and curled as they chased their targets down the corridor.

To gaze at the fiery shapes was to view the arms of the dead clawing their way up from hell. It was like a scene plucked from a nightmare. As if such a thing wasn't frightening enough, the fire was fast, too. The hundreds of arms raced through the air like arrows and clawed after the fleeing women.

Escaping such pursuers required speed on par with Aoi's. With Jeanne and Elaine in tow, Shinobu wasn't going to make it.

"This is bad, Shinobu!" Jeanne cried.

"Th-they're catching up!" Elaine added.

Shinobu, however—

"Don't worry!"

—had a trick up her sleeve.

As they ran, she slammed the butt of her kunai into a particular section of the stone brick wall.

When she did, the brick sank in with a *click*. A moment later, a stone partition dropped from the ceiling between them and the flame.

"Wh-what was that?!"

"We're in the secret basement of a fortress; having traps like that scattered about is a given."

Shinobu didn't just know about the structure's hidden areas—she knew every inch of its construction from top to bottom. Naturally, that included traps, too.

Thanks to Shinobu's immaculate preparation, the three of them managed to get aboveground safely. After emerging into the fort's courtyard, the trio took the stone statue hiding the passageway and returned it to its original position so the flames couldn't follow them.

"Hey! There they are! It's those girls!"

Unfortunately, a search party composed of twenty of Conrad's men immediately spotted them.

"Catch them, dead or alive!"

"""RAAAAAAAAAAAAAAAAH!!!!"""

The soldiers readied their swords and spears at their Bronze Knight leader's orders.

What awful timing. Shinobu clicked her tongue in irritation and drew a flash grenade. Before she had a chance to toss it, however, the ninja sensed something bubbling up from beneath her feet. Something hot.

"EVERYONE, RUUUUUUUN!!!!"

*   *   *

Shinobu had shouted the words at the top of her lungs, as much to her friends as Conrad's men.

"What's she talking abou—? Huh?"

To their own misfortune, the soldiers, who hadn't been privy to the events down below, didn't react in time. A moment later, the earth exploded, and a torrent of flame erupted from underground, swallowing the soldiers whole.

""""AAAAAAAAAAAAAAAAAGH!!!!!!""""

Their fates were the same as Conrad's. The fire refused to take their lives. Even as their bodies turned to cinders, the demonic flames continued to burn them alive. Then, the hellfire moved on to those who'd been fortunate enough to avoid the initial eruption.

"E-eeeeeeeeeeeek!!!!"

"What the hell's going ooooon?!"

"Th-there's arms coming out of the flaaaAAAAAAARGH!!!!"

It grabbed the shoulders, necks, and legs of the poor men and began working its way through their bodies in turn. Eventually, the blaze grew unsatisfied with just the courtyard alone.

The fire split into hundreds of arms, then surged in through every window and opening in Uranus. Every occupant of the fortress was set aflame, and in the blink of an eye, the entire building was burning. As the fires rose, so too did screams from the people roasting alive within it.

Soldiers who wanted to go out on their own terms leaped from the windows one after another and toppled to the courtyard below. The lucky ones died, while others jumped from too low a height or lost their nerve before making the jump. Least fortunate of all were those whose falls should have been fatal, but they somehow survived. For any who yet drew breath, the horror was just beginning.

Even with their bodies charred to the bone, their senses remained unaffected. The burning agony never went away. All they could do was writhe on the ground like worms and beg desperately for death. The sheer malice of the spectacle drove Jeanne to tears. Moments ago, these were people who had been trying to kill her, and yet…

Nobody deserves to suffer a fate like that…! Jeanne could only ponder at how anyone could be so cruel. Even Gustav himself was human. Surely, he realized how much pain he was causing.

Unable to comprehend how one man was capable of such wicked things, Jeanne cried out with tears in her eyes, "Don't stop running! The flames will chase you! Run! Get away from Uranus!! You all need to ruuuun!!"

Meanwhile, Elaine, who'd thought fast on her feet, returned from her stop to the stables.

"Mistress, I brought horses!! Please get on!"

"Good thinkin', Elaine! Jeanne, c'mon!" Shinobu leaped atop one of the horses and called out to her friend.

"AHHHHH… IT BUUUUUUURNS…"

Jeanne remained put, however, staring at the defiled soldiers crawling ever closer.

"Mistress?!"

"PLEEEEEEASE… KILLLLLL ME…"

"———!"

The burning warriors were begging for death.

Honor demanding Jeanne grant those suffering souls an end to their misery, the Silver Knight drew her sword.

"JEAAAAAANE!!!!"

"Ah!"

An earsplitting shout from Shinobu brought Jeanne back to her senses.

"Nobody deserves to die like that, and I get that you wanna help 'em. But there's too many, and we can't save them all! So c'mon…!"

"...Forgive me...!"

Turning away, Jeanne mounted Elaine's steed. As she did, the flames consuming the fort reared and began to give chase, but the horses proved swifter. The three women broke away from the fiery arms and left Fort Uranus behind.

As she raced alongside the few soldiers who'd been fortunate enough to make it out alive, Shinobu pulled out her phone and called Tsukasa over in Dormundt. Thankfully, he answered immediately. Without even letting him say hello, Shinobu frantically explained the situation.

"Tsukes, things just got real ugly over here! Gustav's alive! Yeah! Plus, I dunno how, but he got way stronger since the last time we fought! The Blue Brigade members in the fort were wiped out! A couple of 'em made it out with us, but given what Gustav is like now, you need to get ready for another Rage Soleil, or— Huh? Whaddaya... WHAT?!"

A look of shock crossed the ninja-journalist's face.

"Shinobu?" Concerned for her friend, Jeanne rode up beside Shinobu, but she made a gesture for Jeanne not to worry about it.

"...Sure. That's probably the only real option. Get it done!" With a tap, Shinobu ended the call.

"Who were you speaking to just now?" Jeanne wore a puzzled look. To people of a more primitive world, it must have looked like Shinobu was talking to herself.

"I'll explain later," Shinobu replied. "For now, we need to get everyone as far away from here as possible. Let's see...over that hill should do it!"

"V-very well!" Jeanne agreed.

Their plan set, they drove the confused soldiers away from Fort Uranus.

"Aghhhhhh…"

"Kill…me… Please…kill…me…alreadyyyyy…"

Fort Uranus burned in magic fire. Soldiers crawled around the courtyard. Though their bodies were little more than skeletal frames now, death refused to claim them. Gustav stood among them, gazing at the fort's open gate and licking his lips.

"Hmph. Some of the rats escaped?" He didn't seem concerned in the slightest, however. His foes fleeing was but a trifling matter.

After Gustav had scuttled his way to Drachen, Neuro had embedded a chunk of some obsidian-colored stone in his chest.

"Hraaaaaaagh!"

Gustav drew out more power from the protruding bit of rock.

Give me fire, Gustav demanded. *Summon unto me blazing flames and bind them into spears of calamity.*

The spirits, forced to obey, molded themselves into four red spears. Each was identical to the Rage Soleil Gustav had used to burn a quarter of Dormundt to the ground.

"Fwa-ha-ha-ha! It boils! It seethes! Look at how many spirits this power can bind at once! Incredible…! With this, I can fight for His Grace better than ever before! I will serve him with every fiber of my being! There is no greater ecstasy! Ha-ha-ha-ha-ha!!"

As he cackled, Gustav adorned the four floating spears with wind spirits.

"It matters not where you run, rats! Archride, Buchwald, Findolph, Gustav…the inferno of my rage will burn every tree and blade of grass in the north to the ground!"

Just as the duke made to hurl his deadly weapons, however, he suddenly paused.

"Hmm?"

When he looked up into air, Gustav saw something strange descending from the crimson-stained night sky.

"What's that?" he grumbled.

There was something white shining up above the light from his flames.

A star? That must be it. It must be a shooting star, thought Gustav. If that was true, it was the strangest one he'd ever seen. Never in his life had Gustav borne witness to one that moved so quickly, nor one that looked to be growing gradually larger.

What's going on here? Gustav strained his eyes to look at the thing approaching him. Now that it was closer, it appeared to be a pillar. What he'd thought to be a falling star was actually a jet of flame spurting from the back end of the post. Gustav recognized the object.

Didn't one of those things destroy my Rage Soleil back in Dormundt—?

Just as the Fastidious Duke recalled what the object was, a surge of light and wind took all the rocks, trees, lives, sounds, and color—and annihilated them.

""""Hwaaaaaaaaaaaah?!""""

As Shinobu, Jeanne, and the surviving soldiers crested the hill in their desperate retreat from the flaming hands, an intense wave of sound struck them from behind with all the impact of a physical object.

"Wh-what was that?! Did something explode?!"

"H-hey! Look, there!"

Everyone turned around and stared in blank, abject shock.

While they'd all fled a good distance, Fort Uranus should've still been visible. The far visage of the mighty structure was gone, however.

In its place was a gigantic mushroom-shaped cloud of smoke that climbed into the sky.

"What…what is that thing…?"

"I've never seen an explosion that big…"

"What the hell's going on over there…?"

Soldiers trembled in fear.

However, the true terror came a bit later, when the mushroom cloud dissipated. Not a piece of Fort Uranus had been left standing. All that remained was a massive crater that had been carved into the ground.

"I—I don't believe it… The entire fort got blown away, down to its foundation…?" Jeanne's voice trembled as she looked down from atop the hill. The power it must have taken to destroy a structure that sturdy was mind-boggling. "I had no idea Gustav's strength had grown to that extent… How are we meant to fight such a man…?"

"Ah, that's not quite it," Shinobu corrected.

"Pardon?"

"That explosion didn't come from Gustav. We Seven Luminaries did that."

"What…?! *You* caused that explosion?!"

Shinobu shook her head. "My friends back in Findolph did."

"F-Findolph?! All the way up north?!"

"The empire isn't the only one who can launch massively destructive attacks from multiple domains away. If we wanted to, we could blow up the imperial capital in an instant, all while sitting back in Findolph. All we'd need is that nuclear missile."

The destruction wrought by the bomb could be felt all the way over in Port City Laurier.

The earth rumbled and shook. All the townspeople rushed outside

©Sacraneco

to see what was going on, only to gawk at the mushroom cloud off on the distant horizon. High School Prodigy Masato Sanada and the slave girl he'd bought, Roo, were among that crowd, too. They'd come to Laurier to stock up on supplies.

"Look! It's a big mushroom!" Roo declared.

"Ha-ha! Looks like our favorite politician's gone and done it now! Guy's not fuckin' around!"

"Teacher, what is that? Do you know?"

"Yeah. That there's a smoke signal."

"A…smoke signal?"

Masato nodded and gave Roo an evil grin.

"You like gold, right, Li'l Roo?"

"Yup."

"Good answer."

Masato let out a wry laugh and tousled her hair.

"Well, good news. We ain't just gonna be making money anymore. We're gonna be *making* money. Our own money, I mean, and mountains of it. It's the best fun you'll ever have."

Far away from ground zero, in a Dormundt Manufacturing District lab, Ringo viewed the destruction from a targeting satellite. Once the smoke cleared, the image clearly showed that Fort Uranus was gone. All that remained was a blackened crater.

"Direct hit…confirmed."

After making sure of that, Ringo turned to Tsukasa and told him the news. He nodded and thanked her.

"Shinobu reported the same thing. The operation was successful. Thank you, Ringo. Now, all the preparations to form our republic are in place."

However, her reaction to his gratitude wasn't quite what Tsukasa was looking for.

"…Yeah."

"You don't seem too happy about it."

Ringo gave him a dejected nod. Ever since he'd asked her to build the nuclear missile, she'd been deeply conflicted.

"Should we really have brought this power…this technology to this world…?"

She was at a moral quandary as an engineer.

In terms of destructive capability, guns and atomic bombs were on completely different levels. A nuke could kill tens of thousands of people with the push of a button. Would the presence of the High School Prodigies bring that world's people anything but misfortune? Ringo wasn't sure of the answer anymore.

"Ringo, do you know what it takes to found a nation?" Tsukasa asked.

"Not…really."

"Nothing at all."

"Huh?"

"To put it another way, all you need is the will to do so. The thing about nation-building, as a concept, is that it's so easy even a child can do it."

"R-really?!"

"When you were a kid, did you ever build a secret base? Hypothetically, if a group of children were to declare that their secret base was an independent nation, it would technically be its own country at that moment. There would be no taxes, no annoying schoolwork, no nagging adults. In their land, the children would be kings. However, if a group of children really did something like that, the world wouldn't just stand idly by.

"Even if they brought enough food with them to hole up for weeks, their parents would call the police, their base would be destroyed, and the children would receive a stern talking-to. With their sovereignty lost, their kingdom would crumble.

"Do you understand what I'm getting at? Founding a realm is easy. But holding on to one takes power."

A country needed manufacturing power to keep itself functional. It needed bargaining power to negotiate with its neighbors. And it needed military power to avoid having to cave to outside forces.

"That war magic that torched Dormundt was a threat to our sovereignty. Once we form our republic, whether we go to war with the empire or reconcile with them, we absolutely need to get them to form an agreement banning the use of large-scale destructive magic like that. To do so…we need to demonstrate that we possess destructive power on par with, if not greater than, that war magic. Otherwise, they'll never agree to our terms. After all, negotiations only work when both parties are on equal footing."

When a nation that had nuclear arms bargained with one that didn't, the former could strong-arm the latter with ease. The more powerful side always came away from the table with more. It was impossible for the strong and the weak to coexist on equal terms. The weapons changed with the era, but that law had remained ironclad throughout history. Not once had it been usurped.

As Japan's prime minister, Tsukasa had seen proof of as much, firsthand. That was why he was able to speak with confidence. Humanity would never relinquish power; it was something the species was incapable of.

"By retaliating on Gustav for his use of war magic, we've demonstrated both our power and our propensity for retribution. This was the best outcome possible. Now we've opened the path for negotiations with the empire. So…"

"…!"

Tsukasa paused for a second and squeezed Ringo's hands tight in his own.

"...I believe that this technology will prove to be a blessing for the people of this world."

He spoke with a confident tone and an indomitable smile.

Ah...

For a single moment, however, Ringo saw something else flicker in his eyes. Anyone who'd spent less time with Tsukasa Mikogami wouldn't have noticed it. His words were confident. His expression was dauntless. Behind the strong front he was putting up, anguish and grief were lurking in his eyes. That was when Ringo realized something.

Those pained feelings were what had felt so off about Tsukasa at the end of their date.

Using force to rein in force.

Tsukasa Mikogami blamed himself for being unable to come up with a better option. He didn't think their current outcome was the best one possible—far from it. The young prime minister was a political genius. Undoubtedly, he believed himself capable of coming up with a way to stage a revolution that didn't involve such violence. This was a young man tormented by his own powerlessness, yet he never allowed it to show.

Any doubt or hesitation from Tsukasa would cause the faith of those who looked to him to waver, and he refused to let that happen. He did not allow himself to share his burden with others.

...Ah, I see.

Ringo thought back. She recalled what Tsukasa had said when he first asked her to make the nuclear weapons.

"Ringo...there's something I need you to do."

The request had been framed as an order. Tsukasa had done that intentionally. That way, he could take all the responsibility and blame on himself. It allowed Ringo to hate Tsukasa instead of hating herself. What a sad, lonely sort of strength that was.

Now...I get it.

Back when Ringo had first heard about what Lyrule did, her immediate reaction had been that it would've been impossible for her to do the same. Now, though, she understood. Lyrule had forced her way into Tsukasa's heart.

At the time, Ringo had been shocked at how bold and aggressive Lyrule acted. She'd had it backward, however.

Tsukasa...is a person who mustn't be left alone.

He was of the sort that would shoulder everything on his own, even if it crushed him. Even when the anguish made his heart ache or tempted him to break down and weep, he would continue enduring it in solitude. The only way Tsukasa allowed others in his life was if they reached out and took his hand themselves.

The moment she realized that, Ringo's body moved on its own. She took Tsukasa's right hand, which was still grasping hers, laid her left hand on top of it, and stared into his eyes.

"I don't...hold it against you."

"...!"

She could see that her words had shaken him. Ringo wanted Tsukasa to know that she saw the pain that was eating him up inside. He tried to pull himself together...but Ringo refused to give him a chance to. Her own words were tottering, but her tone was firm, and her gaze was locked straight on him.

"I know...how it is...for you. I know...how hard...you work...to make other people happy. So..." Ringo's grip on Tsukasa's hand tightened. "It's all right...to rely on me more...okay?"

Long ago, Tsukasa had offered Ringo help when she was alone and on the verge of disappearing completely. Now it was her turn to support him, because she loved him. Not once had those feelings ever wavered. It was the strength born from that emotion that let her move past the walls of her anxiety.

A look of surprise crossed Tsukasa's face. The intensity of Ringo's words was out of character for her. A moment later, though, he heaved a self-deprecating sigh.

"...Oh, man. It looks like Winona was right—I'm much worse at keeping secrets than I thought I was."

Back when Lyrule was kidnapped, Winona had been able to see right through him, too. Tsukasa thought it something to be ashamed of. It wasn't right to burden others with his own suffering and internal conflict. As he saw it, it was pathetic.

Tsukasa wondered if perhaps he needed to reconsider himself somewhat. By all accounts, he should've felt mortified, but Ringo's words filled him with joy.

"Thank you. I'm blessed to have such an amazing friend," Tsukasa said from the bottom of his heart. The smile he wore wasn't his usual business one. This time it was an honest reflection of his feelings.

Ringo responded with a slightly disappointed smile...then murmured, "...That's fine, for now."

"What is?" asked Tsukasa.

"Hweh..."

Ringo hadn't meant to say that out loud. After being more assertive than she'd ever been in her life, Ringo's brain must have unconsciously taken the ball and run with it.

Upon realizing that Tsukasa heard her—

"!!!!!!!!!!!!!!!!!!!"

—Ringo went as red as a lobster.

Now that her temporary confidence had worn off and she was back to her normal self, the embarrassment from everything she'd just said, not to mention the physical contact with Tsukasa's hand, hit her like a tidal wave. Ringo couldn't bear to look at his face anymore.

"I—I, um, forgot something! I'd b-better…go get it!"

Frantically pulling away from Tsukasa, Ringo fabricated a flimsy excuse and rushed from the room with her face buried in her hands and steam practically exploding from her head.

As she made her escape, however, the genius inventor was suddenly met with resistance.

"Hwah?!"

The moment Ringo left the room, she slammed into something bouncy and recoiled backward. Whatever it'd been, it was soft and round.

Ringo pried her hands from her face and looked to see what it was. The sight struck her speechless. Standing before Ringo with a pale look on her face…was Lyrule. Ringo's eyes went wide at the unexpected visitor, and Lyrule's lips trembled.

"U-um…I'm sorry! I wasn't trying to peep or anything! Keine asked me to give you a message, and I, um…I happened to spot you two holding hands…and it startled me, so…I-I'm sorry for i-i-interrupting…!"

Lyrule turned and fled, her hair whirling as she ran. The elf girl didn't know what to feel. She'd just come face-to-face with something she'd never suspected. Now that she knew of it, Lyrule wished she could forget. Little droplets cascaded from the corners of her eyes.

In that instant, both girls became fully aware that they had a rival they needed to overcome.

"Oh, goodness. To think they settled things before I could even send in my reinforcements. Can't say I saw that one coming."

In Drachen, atop the imperial castle's highest steeple, Imperial Grandmaster Neuro ul Levias gazed at the light of the explosion and let out a sarcastic laugh.

"That much firepower, though? To kill one man? I suppose that'll serve as a check against our war magic for the time being."

It was clever; Neuro had to concede that much—ruthless as well.

Clearly, the enemy leader was quite the opponent. All it took was a single glance for Neuro to understand Tsukasa's message.

"More importantly, though…those flames are *not of this world.*"

Neuro's dark golden eyes gleamed malevolently as he smiled. He'd had a hunch ever since he'd received word that there was a group calling themselves the Seven Luminaries.

"So, you still insist on standing in our way, Yggdra?"

At that moment, the moon peered out from between the clouds, faintly illuminating the steeple. Neuro's shadow, faint though it was, appeared *decidedly inhuman.*

It wasn't until much later that the High School Prodigies would come to learn that the empire's true darkness was far deeper and more ebon than they could've possibly imagined.

The Order of the Seven Luminaries and the Freyjagard Empire weren't the only ones who witnessed the High School Prodigies' display of might.

"_____"

On the east side of the empire, there was a forbidden forest where

©Sacraneco

none dared to tread. High off the ground, atop the bough of one of its massive trees, a girl sat and gazed off at the horizon. Her hair was darker than the blackest night. She wore a kimono fashioned from red and black cloth and sported a *long pair of ears*. In one hand, she held an elegant *nodachi* greatsword bound by a cord adorned with a decorative bell on its end.

Another young woman climbed after her and called out with a frightened look on her face, "E-eep! It's so high! Lady Kaguya, we're exposed up here! What if the imperials spot us?"

The one apparently named Kaguya didn't turn to look at her companion. Her blue eyes remained fixed on the distant northern horizon.

It was much too far from the blast site to make anything out, but Kaguya could feel it.

She could hear the spirits' commotion.

"The udumbara blooms…"

"Huh?"

Not understanding what Kaguya was saying, her companion voiced her confusion.

Finally, the girl turned and said, "The world is stirring. Hibari, I have a message for you to convey to Shura."

Her declaration was quiet but brimming with conviction.

"Tell her I make for the north."

𐃘 Prophecy of Flame 𐃘

After the Seven Luminaries' long-range strategic nuclear bombing of Oslo el Gustav, there was no one left to oppose them. The Blue Brigade's ruling nobles descended into bitter infighting after having lost their leader, Conrad.

While that went on, Jeanne and the rest of the founding members who still believed in Blumheart's ideals turned their backs on the Blue Brigade and seceded. As they joined the Order of the Seven Luminaries, so did the Gustav domain's general populace. Just as the group had with its first three domains, the High School Prodigies now claimed sovereignty over Gustav. They had made good on their original plan to have all of the north under their control by spring.

With this new domain under their belt, Tsukasa took the opportunity to announce a large gathering in a field just outside Gustav's capital, Millevana.

"We have an important announcement to make that concerns all citizens," he said.

Nearly every resident from Millevana and its surrounding villages was present, despite it raining on the day of the assembly.

"So what's this meeting today gonna be about?"

"Beats me. But the angels said that it was supposed to be really important."

"I gotta say, this weather's kind of a bummer. Why's it gotta rain, today of all days?"

An enormous crowd stood before a stage that had been set up on the grasslands. Impatiently, they all looked around, waiting for whatever the event was to begin.

Thankfully, they didn't have to wait long.

"Fwa-ha-ha-ha-ha! Hark, mortals! You have done well to brave the elements in response to my summons!"

Akatsuki's voice came booming out of the speakers beside the stage.

"But wait—with the power of my miracles, I will now quell this rain! Beeee...HOLD!!"

Akatsuki was shouting loud enough to clip the audio. Just as he had proclaimed, however, the storm began to break, and a stir ran through the throngs of people.

"Huh? Wait, th-the rain..."

"The rain actually stopped?!"

"God's amazing...!"

Cheers of joy and amazement began to erupt from every which way. Everyone was in awe of Akatsuki's ability to seemingly control the basic forces of nature.

Naturally, the prodigy magician hadn't actually done any sorcery or the like. He'd merely taken the satellite Ringo had set up as part of their missile guidance system, had it predict a change in the weather, and then used that knowledge to say something vaguely prophetic. Given that the concept of a satellite was beyond the understanding of those who lived in this world, however, none suspected such a thing.

From their perspective, God Akatsuki had brought about an event beyond human understanding.

"Fwa-ha-ha! A feat like that is child's play for a deity like me! … Now then, with that pesky rain out of the way, let's get this show on the road!"

After using his scientific prophecy to warm up the crowd, Akatsuki moved on to the main topic. All at once, smoke and explosions rocked the stage.

"Aaaaah!!"

"Wh-what's going on?! Did something blow up…?!"

"No, look!"

When the vapors cleared at last, the crowd discovered that the seven High School Prodigies were standing onstage in a row.

"When did they…?!"

"They must have teleported…! I saw God do that to escape from an iron box once!"

Akatsuki, who was standing in the center of the lineup, floated up into the air. He cast his gaze down on the audience as he spoke into his mic.

"Fwa-ha-ha! Your complexions are looking a whole lot better! I hardly recognize you all!"

"It's all thanks to you, God Akatsuki!"

"You saved my grandson… I can never repay you…"

"Oh, thank you… Thank you…"

"Long live the Seven Luminaries!"

"Long live God Akatsuki!"

A chorus of gratitude rose up to the sky.

"I can feel the passion behind your faith. But I didn't gather you here today to receive your thanks and prayers. Today, I have an important divine revelation to deliver to all the people who follow the Seven Luminaries. To do so, I'm speaking directly into the hearts and minds of

every person living in our lands. Now, if any of you are having difficulty hearing me, you should move closer to the nearest amplifying obelisk so you don't miss anything."

Following the script that Tsukasa had laid out, Akatsuki instructed those listening from other locations around the four domains to move closer to their loudspeakers.

"Now then, my loyal angel Tsukasa will deliver the message on my behalf. Take it away!"

"Very well."

Akatsuki proceeded to turn things over to Tsukasa. The white-haired young man stepped in front of the other five Prodigies, then swept his gaze over the assembled masses as he laid out the current state of affairs.

"As many of you are aware, the Blue Brigade, who fought tooth and nail to save you all from Gustav's menace, was obliterated by the empire the other day for daring to believe in a fair and equal society. We firmly oppose such inhumane acts, so we retaliated with Divine Lightning and eliminated the enemy threat.

"The Blue Brigade heroes we lost are forever gone, however. With their ranks diminished and their leader dead, the Blue Brigade is no longer capable of governing the Gustav domain. As such, they've agreed to turn the domain's sovereignty over to the Seven Luminaries.

"With this, the Seven Luminaries now hold power in all four northern territories of the empire—Findolph, Buchwald, Archride, and now Gustav."

Usurping four imperial domains in a mere month or two was an astounding feat, and the crowd let out gasps of amazement. Even a mere six months prior, no one would've believed there was a force capable of striking back against the empire so.

Much to the surprise of everyone, however…

"But we Seven Luminaries and God Akatsuki have no desire to rule

over you. Taking over the domains was merely a means to an end. In the name of equality for all, we want to see you live independently. In order to do that, there's something you need: a nation of your own.

"Not one that belongs to a single man like the Freyjagard Empire, nor one where a handful of nobles do as they please. You need a nation where each and every one of you is your own master, a place where everyone can participate in government—a republic!"

"Repub-lick?"

"What's that?"

"H-hey, don't ask me... Maybe we're all going to be nobles?"

"That can't be right..."

Confusion swept through the onlookers. That, however, was as Tsukasa had expected. Democracy was an alien concept, after all. Expecting the people to understand it immediately was asking far too much. Instead of trying to explain it with words, Tsukasa instead appealed to their experiences.

"I realize you may find this notion confusing. I told you that you would all participate in government, but it's perfectly natural for you not to understand what that means or what's expected of you.

"But think back and remember. Surely you recall the absurd demands you were faced with when a small group of people controlled every aspect of your lives. Surely you remember the injustices. They didn't just take your wealth and your land; they took your families, your lives!

"Was that acceptable?

"Can you stomach the thought of leaving behind a world that cruel for your children?!"

Tsukasa's tone grew fiercer with each sentence, and the assembled mass of people began getting rather worked up as well.

"No way!"

"We never wanna go through that again!"

"That's right—no way!

"But to ensure that, you all have to stand on your own two feet! You all have to take that first step yourselves! Children get bumped and bruised when they learn to walk, and so too will you.

"Now, we angels will give you all the help we can. Everything you need to support yourselves will be provided while you learn to stand on your own. Should you find yourselves lost, we'll guide you back to the path.

"Our teachings will only get you so far, however. None of it will stick unless you first find within yourselves the will to stand. Relying solely on us will only allow new despots to rise and rip out the seeds of equality by the roots."

That would make it all meaningless. Freedom wasn't something to be given. It was something you poured your heart and soul into to win for yourself. When people forgot that, it was all too easy for them to lose their dignity. Above all, one needed to be willing to fight to protect their freedoms with their own two hands.

"And so, I ask you once more! Are you prepared to take responsibility for preserving your freedom and equality?!"

A resounding roar erupted from the crowd.

""""YEAHHHHHHHHHHH!!!!""""

"Are you prepared to fight to protect your rights and dignity?!"

""""YEAHHHHHHHHHHHHHHHHHHHHHHHHHHH!!!!""""

People raised their hands and fists overhead as they cheered. Such united action wasn't limited to Millevana or even the Gustav domain. All throughout Archride, Buchwald, and Findolph, people were doing the same.

Men whose wives and daughters had been violated by their lord, elders who'd watched as egotistical nobles had robbed their beloved families of even the right to smile, parents who wanted their children to inherit the beautiful future the High School Prodigies were offering, all were united.

Save for a few disgruntled ex-nobles, everyone's fists were raised in the air as they cheered. Clenched tight in those hands was the dignity of everyone who had ever suffered under the Freyjagard Empire, and they were never going to let that go.

All that was left was to make it official—to make a pledge to the world.

"Then from this day forth, the Seven Luminaries declare this land to be the independent Republic of Elm—"

At that very same moment...

Huh...?

Lyrule, who was standing beside the stage, suddenly felt a shiver go up her spine. The spirits were stirring, so quietly it was inaudible, yet so loud it felt like her ears were going to burst. They were screaming in fear.

Something is...coming...!

"Beary bad news!!" Bearabbit's voice blared over the loudspeakers, cutting off Tsukasa's declaration of independence. Hurriedly, the AI shouted at the High School Prodigies gathered atop the stage. *"There's an unidentified heat signature bearing down on you at twelve o'clock! It's bearreling straight toward Akatsuki!"*

"WHAAAAAT?!?!"

Akatsuki looked off into the sky, aghast. It was there that he saw a flaming arrow arcing through the air like a dragon. It was headed right for him.

"WHYYYYYYYY?!?!"

The magician's mind went blank at the unexpected display of hostility.

"Akatsuki, drop out of the sky, now!!" Tsukasa demanded.

"—!" The sudden cry of his friend only barely managed to snap

Akatsuki out of his daze. He released the mechanism keeping his body suspended in the air and dropped like a rock back toward the ground.

"Someonnnne catchhh meeeeeee!"

"Oof!"

Masato, the brawniest of the group, reached out his arms and effortlessly caught Akatsuki out of the air.

"You okay, Prince?"

Akatsuki thanked him profusely through fright-induced sobs.

"Hic, thank you, hnf, Masato..."

"Actually, given how I'm carrying you, I guess it should be *Princess*."

"Dammit, jackass, put me down!"

Clearly, Akatsuki was doing just fine.

Watching the exchange filled Tsukasa with relief. Unfortunately, he never got a chance to show it.

""""UWAAAAAAAH!!!!"""""

Screams rose from the crowd as a pillar of flame burst from the ground behind them.

Tsukasa and the others turned to look upon the face of their assailant. The entity stood in the center of the terrified, fleeing audience members. Its form was wreathed in fire, and its armless body was charred so badly it was hardly recognizable as human.

The malevolence and hatred in the creature's eyes were unmistakable, however, even at a distance. Such qualities identified the attacker as surely as anything else could have.

"Oslo el Gustav...," Tsukasa muttered.

It was hard to believe, yet Gustav must have somehow survived a nuclear explosion.

"Kill...emperor's...enemies... Kill... KILL..."

The man charged toward the Prodigies. Even with his mind all but gone, he was still determined to slay his master's foes.

* * *

"■■■■■■■■■■■!!!!"

The scream that came from his mouth was a sound no human throat should ever have been able to make. As it left Gustav's lips, the black jewel embedded in his chest released a wave of dark light as though resonating with the cry.

""""Wh—?!"""""

Then, something horrifying happened. A wave of the same obsidian substance began to spread from the gem, shredding the man's flesh as it propagated across his body. In moments, Gustav now sported a crystalline carapace. The rapid mutations didn't stop there, either.

The stone's corrosion reached even as far as the man's skull, causing black, bull-like horns to sprout from his forehead. The crystals also reconstructed his lost arms, sprouting from the stumps on his shoulders and restoring his body to its former four-limbed glory.

When at last the horrific transformation was complete, Oslo el Gustav looked more like a demon than a human being. In keeping with the comparison, flames began to issue from his body. Once they rose a good forty feet into the air and took on the shape of a colossal humanoid, Gustav dashed straight toward the Prodigies with his fire effigy in tow.

"H-hold your ground! Fire! Shoot him dead!"

The soldiers that the Seven Luminaries had kept on standby rushed to block Gustav's path and showered him with gunshots. Most of the hundreds of bullets evaporated from the heat of the flames before they could reach their target, however. What scant few found purchase were rebuked by the thick armor surrounding Gustav.

"Our bullets aren't working?!"

"GrooooaaaaAAARRRRR!!!!"

""""AAAAAAAAAAAAARGH!!!!"""""

With a sweep of its massive arms, Gustav's flame colossus mowed the soldiers down. As the fiery avatar shredded the guards to pieces, Gustav only pressed his advance, the ground turning to soot in his wake. It was like being marched upon by the Devil himself.

"GAH, G-GAH…GAH…GRAAAAAAAAAAAAH!!!!"

""""Ahhhhhhhhhh!"""""

Boiling, bloody froth spilled from Gustav's gnashing teeth. Even so, he continued toward the Prodigies, unabated. The man's furious fervor had burned away whatever sliver of reason was left in his mind.

The bloodcurdling sight struck the soldiers pale, and they weren't the only ones. Still standing onstage, Tsukasa was overcome with awe and terror at the logic-defying entity before his eyes.

No human could endure that… What is he…? That mineral-like skin looks an awful lot like the hide of that monstrous bear we found in the woods near Elm…

Tsukasa's analysis ability in times of crisis nearly proved to be his own undoing, as his curiosity momentarily got the better of him.

"Tsukasa, m'lord! Pull the soldiers back! They're no match for him!" Thankfully, Aoi's cry brought the young man to the moment at hand.

"I shall take over, that I shall! Their efforts are better spent getting the civilians to safety!"

"Can you handle him?" Tsukasa asked.

"Of course!"

With a nod, Aoi drew her trusty katana Hoozukimaru.

"Aoi!! The jewel…aim for the jewel on his chest!" Lyrule shouted as she suddenly came running out from beneath the stage. "I can feel a dreadful power coming from it…! A great, inhuman evil! That must be what's powering him! Please, destroy that jewel!"

The elf girl's face was pale, her voice was trembling, and her teeth chattered. Aoi dared not to ponder what had instilled such base fear in the young woman, but...

"Understood!"

...she knew that Lyrule's words were worth adhering to.

With a nod, the swordswoman dashed toward Gustav so fast it looked like she was flying.

"Everyone, fall back!! That man is mine, that he is!!"

"Those...who would defy...His Grace...will burn, ■ ■ ■ ■, BUUUUUUUURN!!!!"

"You shan't be burning anyone!"

Gustav charged at Aoi in kind. There was a clear difference in reach, however, and Gustav was the first to strike. His fire giant clenched its fists together overhead, then brought them crashing down like a hammer.

Much to the mad duke's surprise and dismay—

"Too slow!"

"_____?!"

—the attack didn't so much as graze Aoi.

The moment Gustav had launched his attack, Aoi had tilted her body forward. By running almost parallel with the ground, she cut air resistance down to a minimum and accelerated to an even greater speed. Just as the hammer fist strike shattered the ground behind her, Aoi sped past Gustav and loosed a single, mighty slash of her katana.

"My ferocious secret technique—Iron-Cleaving Flash!!!!"

A shattering sound filled the air.

".........!"

What had been fractured and broken wasn't Gustav's obsidian flesh, but Hoozukimaru.

Once Aoi passed him by, Gustav seemed content to ignore her, and he ran toward Akatsuki.

She couldn't stop him...?!

Upon seeing Gustav break past Aoi, Tsukasa gritted his teeth and drew the Colt Government pistol from his suit.

"Merchant, protect Akatsuki! Shinobu, get over here!" Tsukasa barked.

"That shan't be necessary," Aoi declared. "Hoozukimaru is a bewitched blade, imbued with a deep-seated vengeance. It will not perish without leaving its mark."

Gustav was so close to the stage he could practically touch it, but all of a sudden, a fracture carved itself into the stone embedded in Gustav's chest. Then, with a shrill *snap*, it shattered.

"GAH... AH........."

The moment it did, Gustav's flames began to weaken, and the man's movements became visibly stiffer. Sparing no moment for hesitation, Tsukasa unloaded several rounds into Gustav's head.

When at last the magazine was empty—

"_____"

—Gustav finally dropped to his knees.

Without the power from Neuro's crystal, there was nothing to keep Gustav going. His body had died back on the day of the Blue Brigade's attack. The temporary life that the obsidian crystal had provided would soon fade.

As the Fastidious Duke lay there dying, a memory flashed through his mind. It was a nostalgic bit of recollection—the day he'd made his first, and only, true friend.

The city's sky was dyed in deep crimson. Gustav was only a boy. The charred corpse of a noble sat beside him as he huddled in an alleyway.

*   *   *

"C'mon, Gustav. Together, we can change this empire for the better."

A fellow knight trainee from Gustav's class offered him his hand.

They were children, *both* firmly believing that they could save people. Back then, the two thought that the world ought to be a place where everyone could live happily. Oh, what fools they'd been.

For a moment, Gustav wondered why he was wasting his final moments recalling such a thing. The man knew perfectly well why, however.

This boy standing before him as he stood on the precipice of death…had the exact same look in his eyes as…

The moment Gustav faltered and fell, the colossus and the flames surrounding him both vanished. With a crumbling sound, the dark crystal coating his body began to break away, too.

Gustav was motionless, and his head was cast down.

Wondering if the man had finally died, Tsukasa moved in to check.

"…Heh…heh-heh… Ha-ha-ha-ha-ha…" Gustav did not rise to his feet, but his shoulders shook with laughter.

He raised his half-melted face, staring at Tsukasa through his blood- and sweat-soaked bangs. The words he spoke carried rationality he hadn't possessed only moments prior.

"You must be…the leader, yes…?"

"I don't know what you're talking about."

Tsukasa refused to give a straight answer. As far as the Seven Luminaries religion went, Akatsuki was its God. There was no reason to say something that went against that merely to give Gustav the satisfaction of knowing he was right. As he dodged the question, Tsukasa drew his spare magazine and reloaded his pistol.

With scorn plain in his voice, Gustav said, "Heh-heh... Play dumb all you please... I can tell...from your eyes. They're the same as mine and Blumheart's... They're the eyes of one who sees how powerless they are to change man's ways, yet struggles in futility to save them nonetheless... They're the eyes of a cheap imposter."

Tsukasa's expression twitched. It was slight but no less definite. Seemingly deriving amusement from that, Gustav continued.

"You still wish to cling to equality? To suffer in pursuit of that absurd ideal? All while knowing what people are truly capable of?! Surely, you suspect there must be another way! You must know that the more you try to save, the more it all slips through your fingers...?!"

"Shut up..."

Tsukasa was growing uneasy. There was no reason to pay this dying man's words any heed. He readied his pistol once more and placed his finger on the trigger...

"Such hubris—and from a common imposter. *We* cannot save anyone."

But Gustav's words got through anyway.

"_____"

Try though he did, Tsukasa was unable to ignore what the duke said. Everything in his body was screaming at him to pull the trigger, but there was something that told Tsukasa that *Gustav's words were true* and that ignoring them was folly. The war between his emotions and his mind froze him in place.

When Gustav spoke next, *his voice rang with pity.*

"In time, you too will learn that this world exists for one man alone. Not an imposter—a *genius, chosen by the heavens to rule*!

"The day you learn that, you too will kneel before the emperor."

"…!"

Cracks spread across Gustav's entire body, and he crumbled away into dust. The wind carried the man's remains on the breeze, and they vanished into the sky. Such was the end of Fastidious Duke Oslo el Gustav.

All that was left of him now was an ominous prophecy about the future that awaited the High School Prodigies—Tsukasa Mikogami, most of all.

AFTERWORD

Thank you for reading *High School Prodigies*, Volume 3, through to the end.

I'm Riku Misora, the author.

It's gotten pretty warm recently.

I've heard it's supposed to get dangerously hot this year, and I live on the second floor of a two-story wooden building, so I'm pretty worried. In the summer, my ceiling is practically a heater. I guess I'll have to break down and buy an air conditioner.

Keine was on the cover this time, and she went on a bit of a rampage, didn't she?

Man, was she scary! Way scarier than she looked on the cover! (LOL)

She's spent a lot of her life on battlefields, so she can definitely hold her own in a fight. Boy, all the Prodigy girls are so strong!

Lyrule also started learning how to use magic, and the Prodigies played their anti-war magic trump card. Next time, their battle against the empire—as well as a foe with deep connections to the world's secrets—will begin in earnest.

I hope you all tag along with the High School Prodigies for their next adventure.

Here at the end, I'd like to thank all the people who helped make this book possible.

To my editor, Kohara, thank you for making revisions and edits up to the last minute with me.

To my illustrator, Sacraneco, thank you for filling another book with cute, sexy, wonderful artwork.

I'd also like to thank Kotaro Yamada, who recently began work on the manga adaptation that's running in *Young Gangan* and *Gangan GA*. It's so exciting! I'm looking forward to reading more of it!

Most importantly, I'd like to express my gratitude to all the readers who've supported this series.

Thank you all, from the bottom of my heart.

I hope we meet again in book four.